I0648165

Josiah Boothby

Statistical Sketch of South Australia

Josiah Boothby

Statistical Sketch of South Australia

ISBN/EAN: 9783337313678

Printed in Europe, USA, Canada, Australia, Japan

Cover: Foto ©Andreas Hilbeck / pixelio.de

More available books at **www.hansebooks.com**

OF

SOUTH AUSTRALIA.

BY

JOSIAH BOOTHBY, Esq., J.P.,

UNDER SECRETARY AND GOVERNMENT STATIST; HONORARY CORRESPONDING MEMBER OF
THE STATISTICAL SOCIETY OF LONDON.

*PUBLISHED BY AUTHORITY OF THE GOVERNMENT
OF SOUTH AUSTRALIA.*

LONDON:
SAMPSON LOW, MARSTON, SEARLE, AND RIVINGTON,
CROWN BUILDINGS, 188 FLEET STREET.

1876.

LONDON :

PRINTED BY WILLIAM CLOWES AND SONS,
STAMFORD STREET AND CHARING CROSS.

CONTENTS.

—◦—

A 2

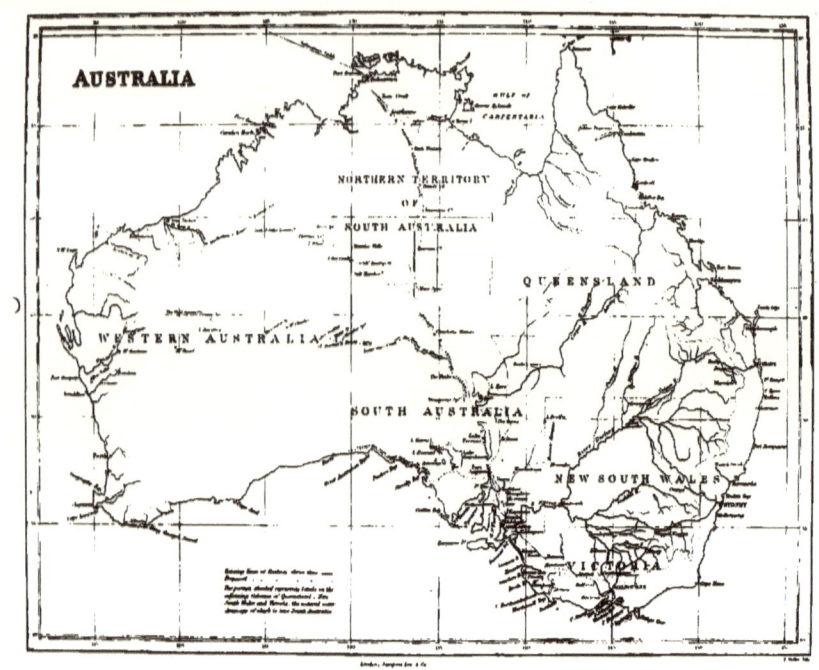

AUSTRALIA

STATISTICAL SKETCH

OF

SOUTH AUSTRALIA.

— •◦• —

THE following paragraphs furnish a statement of facts, based
upon official records, showing the present position of South
Australia, and the progress made from time to time since
her colonization in 1836—not forty years ago. Exhaustless
natural resources, a salubrious climate, indomitable industry
and enterprise in her people, and a freedom and stability
in her institutions, have together placed South Australia in
the high rank she occupies amongst the dependencies of the
British Crown.

GEOGRAPHICAL POSITION.

That portion of the Continent of Australia bounded on the
east by the 141st degree of east longitude, on the north by the
26th degree of south latitude, on the west by the 132nd degree
of east longitude, and on the south by the Southern Ocean,
was constituted a British Province by Act of Parliament 4 & 5
William IV. c. 95, under the designation SOUTH AUSTRALIA.
The area contained within those limits is estimated to be
300,000 square miles, or 192,000,000 acres, nearly twice and a
half that of Great Britain and Ireland. In 1861, the territory
known as "No Man's Land," about 80,000 square miles, lying

between the boundaries of South and Western Australia, was added, by Act 24 and 25 Vict. c. 44, making the western boundary the 129th degree of east longitude.

All the country north of the 26th parallel of south latitude, between the 129th and 138th degrees of east longitude, has also been annexed to South Australia, and is known as the Northern Territory. The present northern boundary is the Indian Ocean, latitude 11° S.; the southern boundary, the Southern Ocean, in latitude 38° S. The Province of South Australia covers twenty-seven degrees of latitude, and twelve degrees of longitude, forming, at present, the largest British colony—the area extending over more than 900,000 square miles.

The northern coast-line included in the before-mentioned limits, starting from the 138th degree of east longitude, about 120 miles west of the Albert River, comprises the western shore of the Gulf of Carpentaria, trending northward to Cape Arnheim; thence west to Port Essington (latitude 11° S.), thence south-west across Van Diemen's Gulf, into which the Adelaide River (Stuart's furthest) flows, opposite Melville Island; and thence to longitude 129° E., Cambridge Gulf, into which, about 100 miles within the boundary, the Victoria River flows. The western boundary is in the 129th degree of east longitude, running from Cambridge Gulf to a point west of the head of the Great Australian Bight, in latitude 32° S., whilst the eastern boundary runs northerly on the 141st degree of east longitude to latitude 26° S., thence west to longitude 138° E., thence north to the Gulf of Carpentaria.

The southern coast-line extends from latitude 38° S. longitude, 141° E. to latitude 31° 45′ S., longitude 129° E., and from its peculiar configuration presents a sea-board of over 2000 miles in length. Between the eastern boundary, near Cape Northumberland, and Encounter Bay, west of the mouth of the River Murray, the coast is generally low and sandy. There are, however, excellent shipping places available for large vessels — among them Port Victor, Lacepede Bay, Guichen Bay, Rivoli Bay, and Port MacDonnell. Westward of Spencer's Gulf is a succession of secure harbours, several of large extent, and with good anchorage for ships of considerable tonnage. Port Lincoln, Smoky, Denial, Venus, Streaky, and Fowler's Bays are important shipping places to the westward.

The coast-line is also deeply indented by two large gulfs—the eastern, St. Vincent's Gulf, running inland to the northward for eighty-five miles, and the larger, Spencer's Gulf, running N.N.E. towards the heart of the colony for one hundred and eighty miles. These gulfs have a mean breadth of thirty and fifty miles respectively, and both taper towards their northern ends. St. Vincent's Gulf is sheltered by Kangaroo Island, ninety miles in length, which lies to the southward of it, leaving two fine entrances, one from the westward through Investigator's Straits, twenty-eight miles broad, and the other from the eastward through Backstairs Passage, eight miles in width.

The principal agricultural and mineral districts of the Colony are contiguous to the two gulfs, the shores of which are seven hundred and eighty miles in length, the greater part being entirely protected from the ocean swell. Numerous outports and shipping places, of which there are over fifty, enable settlers to ship their produce at a very small cost. These gulfs are divided by Yorke's Peninsula, some one hundred and twenty miles long, and twenty miles broad, having large tracts of wheat-growing land, and the principal seat of mining industry.

Situate on the eastern side of St. Vincent's Gulf are the following ports :—Ports Adelaide, Glenelg, Wakefield, Willunga, Noarlunga, and Yankalilla ; and on the west, or peninsula side, shipping places at Edithburg, Stansbury, and Ardrossan. The eastern side of Spencer's Gulf is supplied by Ports Moonta, Wallaroo, Broughton, Pirie, and Port Augusta at the head of the gulf, while Franklin Harbour, Tunby Bay, and Port Lincoln, are on the western side of the same gulf.

A mountain range commences at Cape Jervis, at the eastern entrance to Gulf St. Vincent, and extends in a northerly direction, averaging some thirty miles in breadth, and dividing the waters flowing eastwards into the River Murray and lakes, and westwards into the gulf. The highest point is Mount Lofty, after which the range is named, having an elevation of 2334 feet above sea level. Descending rapidly on the western side, marked by numerous glens and valleys for about three miles, it declines gently over the extensive Adelaide Plains for five miles, to the capital, from thence a plain of six miles (almost level) stretches to the sea-coast.

Opposite the north end of the gulf the range separates into parallel ridges, divided by fertile plains of an average width of eight miles.

On the eastern side of Spencer's Gulf, and about ten miles from its shore, the Hummocks and Flinders Ranges rise to a considerable height, Mounts Remarkable, Brown, and Arden, and other points, being about 3000 feet above the level of the sea. From the head of the gulf the range sweeps easterly and then northerly, and forms a chain of hills extending to latitude 29° 30'. This chain, however, separates into distinct ridges, with wide valleys, generally north and south, intervening. In the south-eastern portion of the Colony there are several volcanic craters, Mounts Gambier and Schanck being the most remarkable; the former being 900 feet high, and having at its base soil of the richest description. Throughout the remainder of the district are low ridges parallel to the coast, with intervening swamps and plains.

ADELAIDE, the capital of the Province, is situate about five miles from the eastern shore of St. Vincent's Gulf, in latitude 34° 57' S. and longitude 138° 38' E., and PORT ADELAIDE, the principal port, is about seven miles north-west from the City, and connected therewith by rail.

GENERAL GOVERNMENT.

The Constitution granted to South Australia by Her Majesty, by virtue of Imperial Act 13 and 14 Victoria, c. 59, was proclaimed on the 24th October 1856, on which day the

Queen's assent to the Constitution Act, No. 2 of 1855-6, was received in the Colony. Under that Statute the Parliament consists of two Houses—the Legislative Council and the House of Assembly—the former being composed of eighteen members, and the latter, at that time, of thirty-six. In 1873 the electoral districts of the House of Assembly were increased from eighteen to twenty-two, and the number of members from thirty-six to forty-six.

The Legislative Council, which cannot be dissolved by the Governor, is elected by ballot, the whole Province forming one electoral district for that purpose. Each member is elected for twelve years; and every four years the six members who have been longest on the roll of the Council retire. The qualification for a member of the Legislative Council is that he shall have attained the age of thirty years, that he is a subject of the Queen, and that he has resided in the Province for three years. The qualification of a voter for this branch of the Legislature is that he shall be twenty-one years of age, a natural-born or naturalized subject of Her Majesty, and have been on the electoral roll for a period of six months. He must also either be possessed of a freehold of the value of fifty pounds, or of a leasehold of the annual value of twenty pounds, having three years to run, or with right of purchase; or be in occupation of a dwelling-house of the annual rent value of twenty-five pounds. The constitution of the Legislative Council is unaltered by the late amendment of the Electoral Act. The total number of voters for the Legislative Council is 18,445, or forty per cent. of the adult male population.

The House of Assembly, which is liable to dissolution by the Governor, is elected for three years; and of the twenty-two districts represented in it, three return three members each, eighteen two members each, and the other returns one member only. The Constitution Act prescribes no other qualification as necessary for a member of the House of Assembly than that he shall be an elector. An elector's qualification to vote is that he shall be of full age, and have been six months on the electoral roll. The total number of electors on the roll for the Assembly is 34,404, or seventy-five per cent. of the adult male population.

Responsible Government is carried on by six Ministers, members of the Legislature, who form the Cabinet, and who are *ex officio* members of the Executive Council, advising the Crown, in the person of Her Majesty's representative, His Excellency the Governor of the Province.

The following are the titles of the ministerial officers, viz. :—Chief Secretary, Attorney-General, Treasurer, Commissioner of Crown Lands and Immigration, Commissioner of Public Works, and Minister of Agriculture and Education. Each Minister has control over several departments of the public service, the duties of which are conducted by permanent official heads.

LOCAL GOVERNMENT.

Local self-government was established in South Australia as far back as 1840, in which year the Corporation of Adelaide was constituted; but elective Municipal Institutions only became general during the administration of Sir Henry Young. Most beneficial results have flowed from the adoption of the principle. Under it the people have been taught the lesson of self-reliance, and have cheerfully taxed themselves for the prosecution of public works of general utility, over which the local authorities—a Board of from five to seven members elected by and from the ratepayers of the District—exercise control. Although the State supplements pound for pound all sums raised and expended on public works in the District, the Council have in their hands the entire management of such expenditure, and of all municipal affairs. Without such Councils it would have been difficult to introduce into sparsely populated and unsettled districts many of the social and political advantages now enjoyed by people resident at considerable distances from the seat of Government.

Corporations have been established in the principal centres of population to the number of sixteen, and ninety District Councils, constituted throughout the settled districts. The total annual rateable value of property is £1,045,711, of which £391,929 is within the limits of Municipal Corporations, and £653,782 is within the boundaries of District Councils. The usual rate declared upon the assessment is one shilling in the pound sterling. The total revenue of these local bodies in 1874 was £125,351, and the amount expended on works of permanent utility £80,945.

The following return of the aggregate assessments and receipts of the several Municipal Corporations and District Councils, and the amount expended on local improvements, affords a reliable index of the steady settlement of the country during the last ten years :—

Year.			Rateable Annual Value.	Receipts.	Expended on Local Improvement.
			£	£	£
1865 ...	...	...	684,095	75,296	43,185
1870 ...	...	...	920,951	86,499	72,865
1874 ...	...	...	1,045,711	125,351	80,944

Of the total municipal income, about one-fifth was contributed by the State in the shape of grants, and the expenditure on local improvements of a permanent character was two-thirds of the total receipts.

POPULATION.

INHABITANTS.—The population of South Australia at the close of 1875 was estimated to be 210,442 souls. The last Census was taken on 2nd April 1871, on the same day and in the same manner as those of Great Britain and her other Australian Colonies. A general idea of the social condition of the people at the present time may be gathered from a review of the chief points then inquired into, bearing in mind the fact that whilst the number of the population has increased by one-third, a more than proportionate advance has been made in industrial progress, material wealth, and social prosperity. Altogether seven enumerations have taken place since the establishment of the Colony—latterly at intervals of five years—as shown in the following table :—

Date of Enumeration.	Males.	Females.	Total.
1844. February 26...	9,526	7,840	17,366
1846. February 26...	12,670	9,720	20,390
1851. January 1	35,302	28,398	63,700
1855. March 31	43,720	42,101	85,821
1861. April 8	65,048	61,782	126,830
1866. March 26	85,334	78,118	163,452
1871. April 2	95,408	90,218	185,626
1875. December 31 (estimated)	107,944	102,498	210,442

In the foregoing table the aborigines are not included. At the Census of 1871 they numbered 3369, so far as could be ascertained.

It will be observed that during the last ten years there has been a numerical increase of population to the extent of 46,990, or nearly one-third. The total population enumerated in 1871 was 185,626, of which 95,804 were male, and 90,218 females. The number at the close of 1875 is estimated, as before said, to be 210,442, namely, 107,944 males and 102,498 females. So close an approximation to equality in the numbers of the sexes is highly satisfactory, and testifies to the settled character of the people.

DISTRIBUTION.—One of the most important facts brought out by the Census is the way in which the population is distributed throughout the country. A frequent review of the movements of the people is essential to the carrying on of the duties of Government in a country where settlement advances so rapidly that centres of population arise where but a few years before sheep only depastured.

The returns under this head are exceedingly satisfactory, as showing that eighty-five per cent. of the whole number of the people are resident in the country districts, and employed directly or indirectly in the cultivation of the soil, or in the production of mineral and pastoral wealth. Since 1861 the residents in the city have increased from 18,303 to 27,208, or by forty-eight per cent. During the same ten years the settlers in the country districts have increased from 108,527 to 158,413, or by forty-six per cent.

The table on page 14 shows the number of inhabitants, the number of males and females, the number of houses, and the number of adult males in each county, and in the Province, at the date of the Census of 1861 and of 1871.

In a country where so large a proportion of the people is engaged in agricultural and kindred pursuits, population must be widely distributed. There are, however, in addition to the City of Adelaide, with a present population of over 30,000 (exclusive of suburbs, which may be computed at as many more), other populous townships, viz. Kensington and Norwood, with 5132 inhabitants; Moonta, 4775; Hindmarsh, 3221; Port Adelaide, 2482; Kapunda, 2273; Wallaroo, 1983; Kadina, 1855; Gawler, 1652; Gambierton, 1604; Kooringa, 1561, Glenelg, 1324; and Clare, 1004. There are 20 townships with between 500 and 1000, and 60 with between 200 and 500, and some 150 villages with an average of less than 200 inhabitants.

BIRTH-PLACES.—The returns showing the birth-places of the people indicate a steady increase in the number of the South Australian born and of British birth, as well as, in a lesser degree, of those from British possessions other than the United Kingdom. The native-born element, of course, preponderates, forming 55 per cent. of the population; the next largest class being persons of English birth, who form twenty-five per cent. Ireland has contributed eight per cent., and Germany and Scotland each 4·5 per cent. The proportion of males and females in the settled districts is about equal. There are more English men than English women, and more Irish women than Irish men. Out of 8309 Germans, 4681 are males and 3628 females. Of the 185,626 enumerated in 1871, 102,676 were native-born, 46,752 were of English birth, 14,255 came from Ireland, 8309 from Germany, 8167 from Scotland, 3469 from other British possessions, and 1356 from other foreign States. The children of German and other colonists from foreign countries are returned as South Australians.

Counties and Pastoral Districts	Persons 1861	Persons 1871	Males 1861	Males 1871	Females 1861	Females 1871	Houses 1861	Houses 1871	Adult Males 1861	Adult Males 1871
Counties—										
Adelaide	66,238	85,593	32,075	41,454	34,163	44,139	15,292	18,600	14,365	18,318
Gawler	3,784	8,660	1,959	4,715	1,825	3,915	874	1,658	846	2,101
Light	14,980	20,019	7,835	10,329	7,145	9,690	3,036	3,811	3,574	4,546
Stanley	4,835	9,785	2,506	5,301	2,329	4,484	924	1,818	1,130	2,407
Victoria	538	818	320	515	218	303	174	159	200	279
Daly	1,232	12,353	863	6,510	369	5,813	312	2,574	501	2,864
Fergusson	...	576	...	377	...	199	...	122	...	221
Frome	989	1,839	550	939	439	900	273	331	335	438
Hindmarsh	12,502	13,562	6,457	6,857	6,045	6,705	2,542	2,730	2,712	2,651
Sturt	4,546	5,730	2,403	2,912	2,143	2,788	888	1,103	1,015	1,139
Eyre	1,097	2,332	595	1,275	502	1,057	232	457	265	516
Burra	5,483	3,401	2,882	1,750	2,601	1,651	1,225	877	1,348	777
Young	52	80	30	40	22	40	10	14	22	23
Hamley	...	72	...	52	...	20	...	15	...	31
Albert	69	75	42	43	27	32	17	13	19	23
Alfred	...	72	...	47	...	25	...	10	...	26
Russell	257	793	154	457	103	336	60	136	82	211
Cardwell	...	109	...	72	...	37	...	26	...	39
Buckingham	...	228	...	122	...	106	...	42	...	58
MacDonnell	652	779	416	460	236	319	136	184	253	238
Robe	1,477	2,407	816	1,371	661	1,036	250	452	462	672
Grey	3,337	9,445	1,870	5,037	1,467	4,408	610	1,816	1,018	2,346
Flinders	738	1,551	431	823	324	728	217	305	234	369
Total of Counties	122,826	180,279	62,207	91,488	60,619	88,791	27,102	37,284	28,471	40,343
Pastoral Districts	3,376	4,584	2,285	3,218	1,091	1,366	802	1,032	1,430	2,212
Shipping	628	562	556	530	72	32	...	...	476	423
Northern Territory	...	201	...	172	...	29	...	17	...	146
Grand Total of South Australia	126,830	185,626	65,018	95,408	61,782	90,218	27,904	38,333	30,377	43,124

CONJUGAL CONDITION.—With reference to the conjugal state, there were, in 1871, 30,002 married males and 30,029 married females. Married women exceed in number the married men in towns, and the reverse is the case in the country districts, where also bachelors predominate. The proportion of bachelors to spinsters at marriageable ages (all above fifteen), is as twenty-one to fifteen, but of adults as eleven to five. The following table shows the number of married, unmarried, and widowed persons, males and females, of the age of fifteen and upwards :—

		Number.
Unmarried	Bachelors	21,638
	Spinsters	15,179
Married	Husbands	30,002
	Wives	30,029
Widowed	Widowers	1,571
	Widows	3,521

AGES.—The proportion in which the number of males and females at the under-mentioned periods of age stood to the total of the Province is as follows :—

AGES.	The Colony.			City of Adelaide.			Rural Pastoral Districts and Shipping.		
	Persons.	Males.	Females.	Persons.	Males.	Females.	Persons.	Males.	Females.
All ages	185,626	95,408	90,218	27,208	12,699	14,509	158,418	82,709	75,709
Under 5	31,450	15,920	15,530	3,992	1,983	2,009	27,458	13,937	13,521
5 and under 15	52,237	26,277	25,960	6,950	3,340	3,610	46,287	22,937	22,350
15 and under 21	20,625	10,088	10,537	3,249	1,350	1,899	17,376	8,738	8,638
21 and upwards	81,141	43,003	38,138	12,997	6,012	6,985	68,144	36,991	31,153

From the above statement it will be seen that in a population of 185,626 souls, seventeen per cent. were infants under five, twenty-eight per cent. were children under fifteen, twelve per cent. youths, and the remaining forty-three per cent. of the whole number were adults.

Taking the number of persons between the ages of fifteen and sixty-five, viz. 98,365, as fairly representing the class upon whom devolves the duty of sustaining the extreme youth and the bulk of the old age of the country, it will be seen that such class forms fifty-three per cent. of the whole population. The man power—that is, all males of fifteen years and upwards

—numbers 51,271, or but twenty-eight per cent. of the whole people ; being three per cent. below the proportion in 1861.

OCCUPATION.—Very full information with regard to the occupations of the people has been obtained at each census, and no returns can be more practically useful than those which show in what direction the labour of the country is chiefly employed. The following classification shows the number under each head in 1871 :—

OCCUPATIONS.	THE PROVINCE.		
	Persons.	Males.	Females.
CLASS			
I. Persons engaged in the general and local government of the colony, police, &c. ...	1,495	1,482	13
II. Professional: persons in the learned professions (with their immediate subordinates) not in the Government service ...	645	644	1
III. Professional: persons engaged in literature, fine arts, and sciences	1,575	765	810
IV. Trading : persons who buy, sell, keep, or lend money on goods	4,301	3,960	341
V. Personal offices: persons engaged in entertaining, clothing, and performing personal offices for man	10,802	2,712	8,090
VI. Manufacturing: persons engaged in art and mechanical productions, and in working and dealing in mineral, vegetable, and animal matters	7,849	7,842	7
VII. Mining: persons engaged in	3,338	3,338	—
VIII. Agricultural, horticultural, and pastoral: persons working land and engaged in growing grain, fruit, animals, and other products	24,224	23,606	618
IX. Carrying : persons engaged in the conveyance of men and goods	2,917	2,915	2
X. Persons dealing in food and drinks	1,732	1,672	60
XI. Miscellaneous pursuits: persons engaged in occupations not embraced in other classes	6,060	5,919	141
XII. Independent means : persons of property or rank not returned under any office or occupation	543	368	175
XIII. Persons engaged in domestic offices or duties, and of no specified occupation, scholars, &c.	117,766	38,262	79,504
XIV. Persons maintained at public cost or by the community	944	620	324
XV. Persons whose pursuits have not been specified, or were unemployed, &c.	1,435	1,303	132
Total of the population	185,626	95,408	90,218

Agricultural, pastoral, and horticultural pursuits are those upon which the labour of the majority of the industrial population is bestowed, the number actually engaged therein being 24,224, or forty-three per cent. of the specified occupations of males.

Mining is the next prominent branch of industry. Its importance cannot be judged of by the comparatively small number of persons returned as directly engaged in it. The great extent and richness of our mineral properties afford profitable employment to large numbers of artisans, mechanics, and others, who are returned under the headings "Trades" and "Manufactures," but who are in fact dependant upon the prosecution of mining industry. The total number of miners was 3338 in 1871, 1504 in 1861, and 840 in 1855.

The next most important class of manufacturers, persons engaged in art and mechanical productions and working and dealing in mineral, vegetable, and animal matters, numbers 7849, of whom only seven are females.

The next class in point of importance are persons, chiefly females, engaged in entertaining, clothing, and performing personal offices for man, numbering altogether 10,802.

The trading class amounts to 4301; persons engaged in conveying men and goods, 2917; persons dealing in food and drink, 1732; professional persons engaged in literature and the fine arts, 1575; persons in the learned professions, 645; persons engaged in the general and local Government, police, &c., 1495; persons engaged in miscellaneous occupations not enumerated in the above classes, 6060; and the residue of the population, 120,688, composed chiefly of persons engaged in domestic duties, scholars, &c., including those whose pursuits have not been specified and also persons of independent means.

The following table shows the occupations of the population and the number of persons engaged in them, arranged in numerical order :—

MALES.

Occupation.	Number.
Farm labourers and servants	11,128
Farmers	8,531
Labourers (branch of labour undefined)	5,013
Overseers on stations, stockmen, shepherds, hutkeepers, station labourers	2,500
Miners—Copper 2,100	
Carters, slabbers, engine-drivers, stokers, and others on mines 530	
Gold 319	
Smelters, ore-dressers, &c.... 223	
Miners and diggers (otherwise undefined) ... 124	
Lead 42	
	3,338
Commercial clerks, assistants in shops, storemen, &c.	2,057
Builders, carpenters, building surveyors, timber merchants, sawyers, &c.	1,786
Blacksmiths, whitesmiths, founders, mechanical engineers, &c....	1,682
Tailors, shoemakers, dressmakers, outfitters, hatters, &c. ...	1,439
Shop and storekeepers, warehousemen, dealers, hawkers, &c. ...	1,200
Other artisans and mechanics—printers, bookbinders, coopers, &c.	1,162
Masons, bricklayers, slaters, hodmen, stucco-men, &c.	1,137
Carriers, draymen, bullock-drivers on roads, lightermen, &c. ...	1,108
Engaged in sea navigation—sailors, ship stewards, &c.	927
Horticultural—market gardeners, gardeners (master), &c. ...	867
Vegetable food chiefly and drinks—bakers, confectioners, green-grocers, &c.	840
Animal food chiefly—butchers, poulterers, fishmongers, &c. ...	832
Domestic servants (general)—cooks, coachmen, grooms (private servants)	791
Quarrymen, brickmakers, road and railway labourers, &c. ...	726
Workmen in Government employment—messengers, office-keepers, chainmen in survey parties, telegraph constructors, &c.	664
Other occupations—proprietors of labour markets, billiard-table keepers, &c.	594
Owners and drivers of coaches, cabs, watermen, &c.	555
Officers of general government—judges, resident magistrates, government clerks, surveyors, &c.	524
Bankers, brokers, accountants, auctioneers, commission agents, &c.	499
Coach and cart makers, wheelwrights, implement makers, &c....	493
Inn and lodging-house keepers, inn servants, &c.	482
Teachers, schoolmasters, tutors, &c.	405
Pastoral—squatters, stockholders, graziers, sheepfarmers, &c. ...	393
Woodsplitters, fencers, bushmen (otherwise undefined), &c. ...	312
Cabinetmakers, furniture dealers, carvers and gilders, turners, &c.	299
Tanners, fellmongers, soapboilers, woolsorters, charcoal burners, &c.	249
Clergy, ministers, priests, missionaries and their subordinates, pew-openers, &c.	245
Other professions—authors, editors, reporters, photographers, musicians, &c.	237
Police, wardens, turnkeys, &c.	217
Annuitants, independent means, &c.	211
Merchants, importers, &c.	204
Porters and messengers (not assistants in shops or stores) ...	171
Contractors (branch undefined)	160
Carried forward	53,978

Occupation.				Number.
Brought forward	...	...	...	53,978
Vignerons, dressers, gardeners, &c....	...	...	...	154
Woodcutters, water-carriers, woodmen, &c.	...	...	...	154
Overseers (branch of labour undefined)	...	...	...	148
Physicians, surgeons, oculists, dentists, &c.	...	...	...	123
Architects, civil engineers, surveyors (land), draughtsmen, &c.				123
Dispensing chemists, druggists, &c.	...	...	...	96
Lawyers, barristers, attorneys, conveyancers, &c....	...	...	90
Persons deriving income from houses—householders, house proprietors, &c.	...	...	...	87
Law clerks, law stationers, bailiffs, &c.	...	...	...	80
Officers of corporations, district councils, &c.	...	...	...	77
Gentlemen (not otherwise defined) ...	...	...	...	70
Cattle-dealers and saleyard keepers, farriers, poundkeepers, &c.				33
Church officers, vergers, sextons, &c.	...	...	...	10
				55,223

RESIDUE OF THE MALE POPULATION.

Children, relatives, visitors, &c. (not otherwise defined)...	...	...	23,526
Scholars, whether in public or private schools, or at home	...	14,736
Unemployed, "No occupation at present"...	...	...	...	816
Occupation not stated	...	...	...	...	487
Patients in hospitals, asylums, depots, &c.	...	...	...	419
Prisoners	...	...	...	...	201
				40,185

Total of the male population   95,408

FEMALES.

Occupation.				Number.
Domestic servants (general), cooks, &c.	...	...	...	6,443
Dressmakers, milliners, tailoresses, &c.	...	...	...	1,552
Teachers, schoolmistresses, governesses, music teachers, &c.	...	803
Farm labourers and servants, &c. ...	...	...	...	330
Farmers	...	...	...	...	244
Assistants in shops, &c.	...	...	...	...	170
Shop and store keepers, dealers, hawkers, &c.	...	...	...	161
Other occupations	...	...	...	...	141
Annuitants, independent means, &c.	...	...	...	117
Inn and lodging-house keepers, inn servants, &c.	...	...	95
Persons deriving income from houses—house proprietors, &c. ...	38
Vegetable food chiefly and drinks—bakers, confectioners, greengrocers, &c.	...	...	...	32
Animal food chiefly—butchers, poulterers, fishmongers, &c.	...	28
Ladies (not otherwise described)	...	...	...	20
Horticultural—market gardeners, &c.	...	...	...	18
Shepherds' wives assisting as hutkeepers, &c.	...	...	11
Vignerons, dressers, &c.	...	...	...	...	9
In Government employment — office keepers, nurses, &c.	...	8
Other professions — authors, musicians, &c.	...	...	...	7
Merchants, importers, &c.	...	...	...	...	6
Pastoral — squatters, stockholders, graziers, sheepfarmers, &c....	6
Registry office keepers, &c. ...	...	...	...	4
In Government employment	...	...	...	...	3
Employed by corporation — office keepers, &c.	...	...	2
Other artisans and mechanics — bookbinders, &c.	...	...	2
Chemist and druggist (proprietor) ...	...	...	...	1
Mason (ditto) ...	...	...	...	...	1
Blacksmith (ditto)	...	...	...	...	1

Carried forward   10,253

Occupation.							Number.	
Brought forward	...	...	...			...	10,253	
Builder (proprietor)	...	...	...	...	...	...	1	
Cabinetmaker (ditto)	...	...	...	...	...	...	1	
Tanner, &c. (ditto) ...	...	...	...	...	...	...	1	
Wood and water carter	..	...	...	...	...	...	1	
Porter and messenger	...	...	...	...	...	...	1	
								10,258

Residue of the Female Population.

		Number.
Children, relatives, visitors, &c. (not otherwise defined)	...	34,826
Wives, widows, &c.	...	30,555
Scholars, whether in public or private schools, or at home	...	14,123
Patients in hospitals, asylums, depots, &c.	...	284
Occupations not stated	...	84
Unemployed, "No occupation at present," &c.	...	48
Prisoners	...	40
		79,960

Total of the female population	...	...	...	...	90,218

RELIGIONS OF THE PEOPLE.—The various religious denominations were ascertained at the census taken in 1871, and the numbers in connection with each were found to be as follows:—

		Number.	Per cent. of the Population.
Church of England	... ...	50,849	27·39
Roman Catholic ...	... ...	28,668	15·44
Wesleyan Methodist	... ...	27,075	14·59
Lutheran, German	... ...	15,412	8·30
Presbyterian	... ...	13,371	7·20
Baptist	... ...	8,731	4·70
Primitive Methodist	... ...	8,207	4·42
Congregational or Independent ...	...	7,969	4·29
Bible Christian ...	... ...	7,758	4·18
Christian Brethren	... ...	1,188	·64
Methodist New Connection	... ...	363	·20
Unitarian	... ...	662	·36
Moravian	... ...	210	·11
Society of Friends ...	... ...	92	·05
New Jerusalem Church ...	... ...	137	·07
Jews	... ...	435	·23
Protestants (not otherwise defined)	...	4,753	2·55
Other Religions ...	... ...	508	·27
Object	... ...	5,436	2·92
Not stated	... ...	3,808	2·04

Excluding those cases in which objection was taken to affording the information, or the information was not given, it would appear that about eighty-five per cent. of the whole population are members of Protestant Churches, and the remaining fifteen per cent. are Roman Catholics. The Church of England is represented by twenty-seven per cent., the Wesleyan Methodists by fifteen per cent., the German Lutherans by eight per cent., Presbyterians by seven per cent., and the Congregationalists, Bible Christians, Primitive Methodists, and Baptists each by about five per cent. of the total population.

EDUCATION.—The returns under this head only show the number of persons able to read and write, those able to read only, and those unable to read. Omitting children under five years of age, the proportion of each class is as follows:— Seventy-five per cent. of the population can read and write, fourteen per cent. can only read, and ten per cent. can neither read nor write.

Of the rising youth, say from fifteen to twenty-one years of age, ninety-one per cent. can read and write, six per cent. can read only, and only three per cent. are totally uneducated.

That parents are alive to the necessity of giving their children a degree of education which they, from the circumstances of their early life, were precluded from receiving, is proved from the fact that whilst among the adult population sixty-one in every 1000 are returned as unable to read, the number of youths of both sexes between the ages of fifteen and twenty-one who cannot read is only thirty in every 1000; the numbers specified ten years before being respectively eighty-three in every 1000 adults as against fifty-one in every 1000 youths unable to read.

The following table affords a comparison of the degree of education in the different Australian colonies:—

NAME OF COLONY.	Proportion of every 1000 Children between five and fifteen years of age who could		
	Read and Write.	Read only.	Not Read.
South Australia	576	234	190
Victoria	640	207	154
New South Wales	536	209	255
Queensland	512	246	242

BIRTHS, MARRIAGES, AND DEATHS.

The Province is divided into twenty-eight registration districts for the purpose of recording births and deaths and for the registration of marriages. The number of births registered during 1875, was 7408, namely, males 3774, and

females 3634.　The following tables show the number of births
at quinquennial periods:—

	BIRTHS.		
Years.	Males.	Females.	Total.
1856	2336	2152	4488
1861	2868	2683	5551
1866	3470	3312	6782
1871	3695	3387	7082
1875	3774	3634	7408

The average birth-rate is thirty-seven per thousand of
the population, which compares favourably with the birth-
rate in England and Wales, viz. thirty-three per thousand.
The proportion of births is 104 males to 100 females, or the
same proportion as is recorded at home. The number of
marriages registered in 1875 was 1688.

There is an average of eight marriages per thousand of
the population, being almost identical with the rate in the
Mother Country. The annexed statement shows the number
of marriages solemnized by each denomination in 1866, 1871,
and 1875:—

MARRIAGES.

Solemnized	1866.	1871.	1875.
By the Church of England	325	284	391
„ Roman Catholics ...	183	177	199
„ Lutherans ...	101	82	99
„ Congregational Independents	122	95	110
„ Wesleyans ...	164	178	306
„ Free Church of Scotland	1	3	9
„ Presbyterian	108	88	92
„ Christians ...	14	21	33
„ Baptists ...	47	58	82
„ Bible Christians ...	81	93	109
„ Primitive Methodists	94	107	162
„ Methodist New Connection	6	7	8
„ Moravians ...	1	2	3
„ Unitarians ...	6	6	4
„ Jews ...	3	...	2
„ District Registrars	43	76	76
„ Christian Brethren	...	2	1
„ Mission to Aborigines	...	3	...
„ New Jerusalem Church ...	...	4	2
	1299	1250	1688

The rate of mortality throughout the Province was much higher in 1875 than usual, owing to the prevalence of zymotic diseases—measles and scarlatina—which caused (local diseases supervening) an advance of the death-rate, especially amongst infants and children. The total deaths registered were 2118 males and 1918 females. The following is a table showing the mortality in the years mentioned :—

	DEATHS.		
Years.	Males.	Females.	Total.
1856	658	489	1147
1861	1095	867	1962
1866	1537	1216	2753
1871	1352	1026	2378
1875	2118	1918	4036

Nearly one-half of the mortality is of infants under two years—a rate not so high as rules in England. A larger number of male than of female children die at that period of infancy.

The following table shows the average death-rate for ten years under each class of disease in England and in South Australia :—

	DEATH-RATE PER 1000 OF POPULATION.	
CLASS.	South Australia.	England.
I. Zymotic	4·28	5·19
II. Constitutional	1·68	4·19
III. Local	5·26	8·68
IV. Developmental... ...	2·88	3·60
V. Violent	0·7	0·78
VI. Unspecified	0·34	—
All causes	15·14	22·47

The average death-rate in South Australia is fifteen per thousand, as compared with twenty-two per thousand in England.

IMMIGRATION AND EMIGRATION.

Last year, 6566 persons arrived in South Australia, and 4019 left it, yielding an increase of the population from this source of 2547 persons. During that and the preceding twelve months assisted immigration was resumed by Government after a lapse of several years. The sum voted by Parliament for the introduction of immigrants during the coming year (1876) is £100,000, and the balance of the amount voted for expenditure in 1875, equal to £18,551, is also available for the like purpose. These sums provide a fund sufficient for the introduction of about six thousand adults, or between four and five hundred souls monthly.

When it is considered that during the past five years nearly two and a half millions of acres of land have been taken up for agricultural settlement, a steady and moderate increase of man power, suitable to the requirements of the country, becomes an absolute necessity. Such additional labour will be readily absorbed into the general population without producing any disturbance of social interests. This large augmentation of the area occupied by the farming classes has taken place during a period in which the influx of population from abroad only amounted to 4555 souls.

The following statement shows the total immigration and emigration during each of the past five years, and also the number of immigrants introduced at the public expense :—

Year.	Immigration.			Emigration.			Immigrants at Public Expense.		
	Males.	Females	Total.	Males.	Females.	Total.	Males.	Females.	Total.
1871	1,681	851	2,532	2,037	1,145	3,182	—	—	—
1872	1,604	797	2,401	2,173	1,232	3,405	—	—	—
1873	3,064	1,484	4,548	2,126	1,046	3,172	104	122	226
1874	3,555	2,002	5,557	2,226	1,045	3,271	1,192	960	2,152
1875	4,311	2,255	6,566	2,718	1,301	4,019	1,156	911	2,067
Total...	14,215	7,389	21,604	11,280	5,769	17,049	2,452	1,993	4,445

Government immigration was resumed in 1873 ; since the commencement of which year the balance of immigration over emigration has amounted to 6209 souls, or 1764 more than the number introduced at the expense of the State. It will also be noticed that the proportion of immigrants at their own cost largely increased during the past year.

EDUCATION.

The administration of the public votes for educational purposes, and the control and management of State assisted schools throughout the Province, have been vested, since 1851, in a Central Board of Education.

The number of schools licensed by the Board in 1874 was three hundred and twenty, of which fourteen were within the City of Adelaide, twenty-seven in other corporate towns, and two hundred and seventy-nine in the country districts. Presiding over these schools, were two hundred and seventeen licensed schoolmasters and ninety-eight licensed schoolmistresses. The number of scholars attending was 17,426 ; of whom 9625 were boys, and 7801 girls. The average attendance at all schools was 13,774 for one month ; the average number on the roll at each school was fifty-four, and the average attendance forty-three, whilst the percentage of attendance to the number on the rolls, during one month, was 79.

The following table shows the operations of the Board last year as compared with 1870.

				1870.	1874.
Number of licensed schools	...	...	...	300	320
Number of licensed schoolmasters		...	...	222	217
Number of licensed schoolmistresses	...		...	72	98
Scholars at licensed schools, including destitute children and orphans	Highest number on the monthly roll.			Boys... 8,491 Girls... 6,617 ⎯⎯⎯ 15,108	Boys... 9,625 Girls... 7,801 ⎯⎯⎯ 17,426
Average attendance	...	...	...	11,969	13,773

The expenditure of the Board in 1874 was £29,689, being an advance of £9266 upon that of 1870. The total sum expended in aid of erecting district school-houses has been £22,207. The average amount of school fees paid for each scholar by parents, &c. was 19s. 7¼d. The average expense to the State of each licensed school was £83 10s. 3d.

In addition to schools receiving aid from the Government, there have always existed a large number of private schools with an average attendance of about 7000 scholars.

During the past year, a new Education Act was passed, providing that the future management of public education shall be committed to a Council, with a paid president and staff of officers directly responsible to the Minister of Education—a member of the Cabinet. Mr. Harcus thus describes the nature of the improvements contemplated by the new measure:—"Schools will be established wherever there is a certain number of children of a school age who will pay a moderate fee to the teachers" [viz. 4d. per child per week]. "In addition to the fees, the teachers will be paid by the Government, through the Council, salaries varying from £100 to £300 per annum. Schoolhouses will be provided, and the necessary education material. Grants of public lands will be set apart every year, and placed under the control of the Council, the rents from which will be devoted to school purposes. Four and a half hours each day will be devoted to secular instruction, previous to which the Bible may be read—without note or explanation: practically, the instruction will be secular. All children of school age will be required to be under instruction until a certain standard of attainment (to be fixed by the Council) is reached: so far, the system will be compulsory. Provision is made for the gratuitous instruction of children whose parents can show that they are not able to pay for it; but fees may be enforced in all cases where inability to pay them has not been proved. It will thus be seen that the three great principles of public education which are now so much in vogue are adopted in the Bill, with certain modifications—the education is secular, but not to the exclusion of the Bible; free, to those who cannot afford to pay a small fee; and compulsory, wherever practicable. Provision is also made for the establishment of model and training schools, of Boards of Advice, and for the systematic examination of teachers and their classification according to their attainments and proficiency, and for scholarships."

With a view of showing that Parliament is desirous of

fostering and encouraging the growth of a comprehensive system of public instruction, it may be stated that the following grants of money and land have lately been made :— Towards the expenses of the Education Department, payment of teachers, &c., a yearly sum of £60,000 ; and a like amount for the erection of public school-buildings. One hundred and twenty thousand acres of the public estate were also granted to the Council, and provision made for setting apart 20,000 acres in future years. To the University of Adelaide, lately established, an annual grant of five per cent. on all sums contributed to the University from private sources (at present amounting to over £40,000), and also an endowment of 50,000 acres of land. For the maintenance of Institutes, and for the erection of buildings connected therewith, the sum of £16,000.

The South Australian Institute, established in 1856, contains, under one roof, a Public Library and Museum, a Circulating Library, and a Public Reading and News Room. It has also incorporated with it societies for the promotion and study of Philosophy and the Fine Arts. The Institute is managed by a Board of Governors, and is subsidized by the State. The seventy-five country institutes which the parent institute has affiliated are scattered over the length and breadth of the Province. They are governed by Committees elected by the members of each institute. About twenty possess buildings half the cost of which has, in each case, been defrayed from the public revenue.

The number of volumes in the Library of the South Australian Institute is 18,837 ; the number of subscribers is 715 ; and the number of volumes in circulation during the year, 54,648. In the country institutes, the number of volumes is 42,393 ; the number of members, 2904 ; the aggregate income (exclusive of the Government grant), £3360 ; and the number of volumes circulated during the year has been 76,487.

PUBLIC WORSHIP.

The voluntary principle, or freedom of religion from State assistance and consequent control, was established in South

Australia from the date of its foundation. The beneficial results of its operation under the circumstances of this community may be estimated by the fact that two-thirds of the population are provided with suitable accommodation for the observance of public worship. The number of churches, chapels, rooms, and other buildings used for public worship at the end of 1874 was 876, providing 132,000 sittings, distributed in the proportion shown in the following table :—

Denomination.	Number of Churches or Chapels.	Number of Sittings in such Churches or Chapels.	Number of Rooms and other Buildings, used for Public Worship.	Number of Sittings in such Rooms, &c.
	1874.	1874.	1874.	1874.
Church of England	73	19,452	38	1,273
Church of Scotland	2	150	—	—
Roman Catholics	42	11,500	5	480
Congregationalists or Independents	36	8,400	10	400
Baptists	27	5,725	11	680
Wesleyan Methodists	160	30,296	104	2,000
German Lutherans	31	5,324	8	400
Bible Christians	86	14,000	20	750
Primitive Methodists	106	14,000	41	1,000
Methodist New Connection	2	625	2	90
Free Presbyterian	4	600	4	300
Presbyterian Church of South Australia	15	3,960	13	1,190
Unitarians	1	300	1	100
Moravians	1	200	—	—
Friends, Society of	2	200	—	—
New Jerusalem Church	1	130	—	—
Christians (Brethren, Disciples, &c.)	20	5,000	9	2,450
Hebrews	1	200	—	—
Totals	610	120,062	266	11,113

Ten years ago there were 535 churches, containing 86,000 sittings. The number of Sunday schools in 1874 was 525, attended by 35,671 children, instructed by 4650 teachers, of whom 2200 were male and 2450 female. The average attendance of scholars has been uninterruptedly increasing year by year since 1865, when the number reached 23,739.

CHARITABLE INSTITUTIONS.

Ample provision is made by the state for the relief and support of that helpless section of the community which may be divided into aged and sick, persons mentally infirm, and orphan children.

The Adelaide Hospital is a Government institution, under the management of a Board consisting of professional and non-professional members, who with an efficient staff of officers administer the affairs of the institution. During the year 1874, there were 1806 inmates of the Hospital, of whom 98 died, 1579 were discharged, cured, or relieved, and 129 remained on the last day of the year. The daily average number of patients was 134. There are five hospitals in the country districts, and in addition thereto provision is made for medical attendance on the indigent sick throughout the settled portions of the Colony.

Two hospitals for the insane are also provided by the State, and are conducted on the same principles as similar asylums in the Mother Country, and with great efficiency. For every 100,000 of the population, South Australia has 195 insane persons; England has 226. The total number of cases treated was 464; the daily average number in the asylums was 352; the number of admissions was 106; the number of patients discharged, cured, or relieved, was 81; and the number of deaths was 32. Patients able to maintain themselves are also admitted for treatment upon paying reasonable fees.

The asylum for the relief of infirm and destitute persons not requiring active medical treatment affords assistance to the necessitous. The rule is rigidly followed of excluding from in-door relief any able-bodied person, and out-door relief is only given to males in consequence of sickness—and then only on medical certificate; it being understood that no man capable of working and able to earn his own livelihood should be assisted from the funds of the institution. The cases of widows and orphans, or females deprived of their natural protectors, are exceptionally regarded; and applicants for relief of this class are treated according to circumstances, and receive all necessary assistance. The average number in the asylum of male adults is 175, chiefly infirm and decrepit, and 83 female adults. Seventy-two, principally young children, were maintained in the Industrial Schools connected with this institution. On arriving at a suitable age, the children are placed with or adopted by private families, under what is known as the boarding-out system, under the careful supervision of the department, assisted by a committee of ladies who voluntarily devote the necessary time to overlooking the children's welfare. Some five hundred orphans and neglected children have by these means found comfortable homes, and the system generally is considered to have worked with great success.

The protection of the aborigines and the duty of supplying them with medical comforts in sickness, &c., is performed by a public officer. The welfare of these people has also been attended to by several long-established institutions, mainly supported by voluntary contributions.

Among other benevolent institutions of a private character are the Strangers' Friend's Society, Hebrew Philanthropic Society, Female Refuge, Homœopathic Dispensary; institutions for the relief of the blind, deaf, and dumb; cottage homes for the aged and infirm poor and widows; Convalescent Hospital; Orphan Home, for the reception and training of orphan girls; Prince Alfred's Sailors' Home; and Servants' Home.

Although not strictly coming under the head of charitable institutions, it is desirable to mention that twenty-eight Masonic lodges, English, Irish, and Scotch constitutions, are distributed throughout the Colony.

Friendly Societies have also been for many years in active operation under local legislation, and are firmly established with a large accumulated fund at their disposal. The chief orders of these societies are, I.O.O.F., M.U.; the Ancient Order of Foresters; the U. O. Oddfellows; the Ancient Order of Druids; two Independent Orders of Rechabites, and the Order of Good Templars. The total number of members of Friendly Societies is 15,092; their total income, £42,464; their total expenditure, £35,434; and their total assets amount to £87,250.

ADMINISTRATION OF JUSTICE.

The legal tribunals of the Province consist of a Supreme Court, presided over by the Chief Justice, and two Puisne Judges; the Court of Vice-Admiralty, of which the Chief Justice is Judge; the Court of Insolvency, presided over by a Commissioner; Local Courts of Civil Jurisdiction, presided over by Stipendiary Magistrates; and Police Magistrates' Courts.

Subjoined is a statement of the proceedings in the Supreme Court in its civil jurisdiction, during the years 1865, 1869, and 1874:—

	1865.	1869.	1874.
Common Law—			
No. of Writs issued	710	610	479
No. of Records entered for trial	51	61	35
Total amount for which judgments signed	£12,530	£23,444	£19,390
Equity—			
No. of Bills filed	18	33	30
No. of Claims	9	—	—
No. of Petitions	25	23	27
Testamentary—			
No. of Probates	88	102	167
Amount sworn to	£277,070	£155.267	£394,180
No. of Letters of Administration ...	56	55	89
Amount sworn to	£16,670	£38,860	£57,680
Matrimonial Causes Jurisdiction—			
No. of Cases	14	7	18
Appellate Jurisdiction—			
No. of Special Cases from Insolvency Court	1	1	2
No. of Appeals from Local Courts ...	33	16	16
No. of Writs of Certiorari removing Judgment from Local Court ...	44	56	48
No. of Writs of Habeas Corpus, Mandamus, &c....	6	6	5
No. of Special Cases	4	9	—
No. of Writs of Summons	366	216	159

The number of writs passing through the Sheriff's office during the same years was as follows:—

	1865.	1869.	1874.
Capias ad satis.	17	31	25
Fieri facias	36	35	18
Other writs	15	16	11
Totals	68	82	54

The following table shows the number of insolvencies, assignments, &c., and the amount of liabilities and assets specified in the insolvents' schedules, also taken for the same interval of five years :—

	1865.	1869.	1874.
No. of Adjudications issued—			
On Petition of Creditors...	12	13	23
On Petition of Imprisoned Debtors ...	39	68	67
Of which, in *forma pauperis*... ...	38	67	66
On Petition of Debtors at large ...	58	63	*nil*
Totals	109	144	90
Amount of Liabilities, as shown in the Insolvents' Schedules	£117,482	£75,868	£54,637
Amount of Assets, as shown in the Insolvents' Schedules...	£69,741	£31,605	£19,434
Amount of Deficiency, as shown in the Insolvents' Schedules	£47,741	£44,263	£35,202

Local Courts of civil jurisdiction are established in all the principal towns throughout the Province, and number forty-five. They are arranged in circuits, and are presided over by Stipendiary Magistrates. These courts adjudicate in all personal actions involving amounts up to £100, and in actions of ejectment where the land is under the Real Property Act, and does not exceed £100 in value. A Special and two other Magistrates, or a Special Magistrate and a jury of four, constitute a court of full jurisdiction, and one Special Magistrate a court of limited jurisdiction. The latter does not adjudicate on amounts above £20.

The following return shows the number and extent of proceedings in the Local Courts. The figures given as amount of judgments obtained after hearing do not, of course, represent the whole amount recovered through the agency of these Courts, as a considerable proportion of the claims are settled out of Court after issue of the summons, and do not come on for hearing :—

Claims made in the Local Courts of	Number of Summonses Issued.			Amount of Claims sued for.			Judgments obtained after Hearing.		
	1865.	1869.	1874.	1865.	1869.	1874.	1865.	1869.	1874.
Limited Jurisdiction—				£	£	£			
Up to £5	3,896	5,264	6,674	9,056	11,653	14,432	2,699	3,430	3,345
Above £5 and up to £10	1,434	1,879	1,926	10,251	13,184	14,363	3,345	4,615	3,986
„ £10 „ £20	1,014	1,348	1,318	14,478	19,376	17,985	5,120	6,703	5,460
Full Jurisdiction—									
Above £20 and up to £30	393	610	507	9,388	11,813	12,635	3,419	5,210	4,197
„ £30 „ £50	327	468	369	12,720	18,281	14,265	3,930	6,153	4,809
„ £50 „ £100	248	373	280	18,334	29,490	20,508	5,416	8,789	4,856
„ £100, "by consent"	2	1	—	240	131	—	—	205	—
	7,314	943	11,074	74,524	104,934	94,191	23,931	35,138	26,646

The legal profession numbers eighty-five members; the two branches of barrister and attorney are united. A valuable law library, containing about two thousand volumes, is attached to the Supreme Court.

The criminal records of the Courts are calculated to convey a favourable impression of the law-abiding impulses of the South Australian community, the proportion of serious crimes being exceedingly small. In fact, the "criminal class" may be said to be unknown in South Australia. Following is a statement of the number of convictions in the Supreme Court during the years named:—

	1865.	1869.	1874.
Number of Felonies—			
Against the person	12	17	7
Against property	98	87	53
Total number of Misdemeanours ...	24	17	14
Total	134	121	74

The annual number of convictions in the Supreme Court has averaged during the last three years seventy-two, or only one in three thousand of the population. During the past ten years capital punishment has been inflicted in four instances—amongst them one aborigine suffered the extreme penalty of the law.

The following table shows the number of cases of felony and misdemeanour preliminarily investigated in the Police Courts, and how they were disposed of—whether by committal to the Supreme Court, summary convictions under the Minor Offences Act, conviction of juvenile offenders, or by dismissal of cases:—

How disposed of.	1865.	1869.	1874.
Committed to Supreme Court	197	237	150
Committed to Local Court Full Jurisdiction	79	61	—
Convicted—Minor Offences Act	—	—	150
Convicted—Juvenile Offenders	—	—	22
Cases dismissed	155	207	132
Total	431	505	454

About one-half of the commitments for trial in the Supreme Court resulted in conviction.

In addition to the preliminary investigations above referred to, the Stipendiary Magistrates have summary jurisdiction in cases of breaches of the provisions of Acts of Parliament where the penalty is limited to fine, or to fine and imprisonment. This class of offences is principally composed of cases of drunkenness in the streets, offences under the Police Act, common assaults, breaches of the Waste Lands and Impounding Acts, the Merchant Shipping and Marine Board Acts, and non-compliance with Municipal bylaws.

The following table indicates the number of cases heard and determined in the years 1865, 1869, and 1874:—

	1865.	1869.	1874.
Informations under Acts of Councils, &c.—			
Dismissals	732	749	688
Convictions	2,632	3,129	3,445
Drunkenness ...			
Dismissals	105	86	55
Convictions	1,530	1,540	1,615
Total	4,999	5,504	5,803

Considering the increase of population during the ten years, the relative number of convictions, especially in cases of drunkenness, has materially declined.

LAND TRANSFER, LIENS, MORTGAGES, ETC.

The Statute known as the Real Property Act of South Australia affords a facile and convenient process by which the transfer of landed property may be accomplished in as easy and cheap a manner as any ordinary commercial transaction. Where almost every man is a landowner, or is interested in land—either as vendor or vendee, lessor or lessee, mortgagor or mortgagee—dealings in real estate become a matter of almost everyday occurrence. It may be said to be quite exceptional for an individual in South Australia not to be, more or less, personally interested in the establishment of a

Years	Value of Land brought under operation of Act, including Land Grants.	Totals	Foreclosures	Writs	Orders of Court	Recoveries by Lessors	Assignments, &c. deposited	Withdrawal Caveats	Transmissions, &c.	Licences	Schedules of Trusts	Surrenders of Leases	Transfers of Leases	Encumbrances	Nominations of Trustees	Caveats, &c.	Registration Abstracts	Powers of Attorney	Discharges of Mortgages	Transfers of Mortgages	Leases	Mortgages	Transfers	Applications	Amount Lent on Mortgage
1858	£132,500	263													2	4					1	24	54	184	£5,670
1859	538,340	1,355													10	18	2	1	9	3	50	265	190	829	54,719
1860	508,216	2,031									2	1	1	4	1	15	14		1	48	9	71	530	348	987	178,370
1861	451,475	2,183					2				8	1	4	4	5	1	17		1	155	11	155	558	505	747	213,424
1862	477,502	2,891				1			10	6	7	7	7	9	1		34		4	239	26	174	735	745	901	233,829
1863	505,906	3,598		1		1			22	22	16	16	24	13	5		36		9	325	23	227	901	899	1,060	260,423
1864	623,167	4,406	1	1	1	2			19	58	16	29	31	17	4		34		33	493	40	227	1,200	1,292	1,145	333,401
1865	939,900	5,237			1				20	53	16	15	37	34	2		71		22	605	49	290	1,697	1,767	1,142	492,158
1866	779,648	6,060	2	1	1				22	41	21	19	32	47	5		76		24	708	66	334	1,700	1,934	1,031	677,958
1867	478,890	5,962		7	4				36	63	34	14	87	39	7		47		14	818	189	320	1,837	1,703	817	705,543
1868	518,646	6,117		13	6				20	99	31	22	56	28	9		56		21	975	105	296	1,835	1,771	779	640,114
1869	540,410	6,549		11	12				27	106	36	17	63	36	15		67		15	1,084	106	333	1,725	2,075	812	766,344
1870	427,310	6,101		12	10				38	185	29	22	72	41	13		70		15	929	141	247	1,612	1,387	662	667,470
1871	463,686	6,582	6	9	14				37	198	42	21	79	49	9		42		16	1,198	133	339	1,648	2,044	704	697,223
1872	475,046	7,334	7	12	12	1			36	214	43	22	78	56	29		71		23	1,410	201	335	1,667	2,521	611	642,048
1873	788,576	8,069	12	5	7				16	227	40	21	77	61	6		81		24	1,619	114	357	1,977	3,014	738	699,991
1874	606,050	8,701	5	3	2				28	172	40	15	90	55	9				22	1,561	101	395	2,352	3,334	764	1,068,693
1875	632,102	10,336	2	3	5				27	302	46	20	103	83	16		25		31	1,658	152	413		4,210	830	997,775

simple and inexpensive method of dealing with this description of property. There can be no question that the operation of the measure has been highly advantageous to the community ; and as considerable interest is attached to the working of so important a reform, a detailed statement is given of the transactions of the office in each year since its establishment in 1858. (*See* page 35.) The total value of the lands brought under the operation of this law amounts to nearly ten millions sterling.

An Assurance Fund in connection with the Act was established with a view of meeting claims for compensation on the part of any person who, through error or fraud, might suffer from the carrying out of the principles of absolute indefeasibility of title. This fund is derived from a contribution of one halfpenny in the pound levied on all property brought under the operation of the Act; it now amounts to over £30,000, and is invested in Government securities. The claims on the fund have reached £308 up to the present time.

The following statement shows the number and amount of liens, mortgages, and other securities for advances of money registered during the years mentioned :—

Years.	Mortgages on Land.		Mortgages on Stock.		Liens on Wool.		Bills of Sale, &c.	
	No.	£	No.	£	No.	£	No.	£
1866 ...	2,252	1,033,422	91	266,031	22	51,072	158	130,153
1871 ...	1,922	920,891	151	116,875	36	82,513	259	67,498
1875 ...	2,627	1,289,635	156	254,508	41	55,043	268	168,194

Of the total amount of mortgages on land registered last year, £997,775—or three-fourths of the whole—were advances upon land under the operation of the Real Property Act.

REVENUE AND EXPENDITURE.

The finances of the Colony of South Australia have never been in a more prosperous condition than at present. The returns of receipts from all sources of revenue indicate the steady progress and growth of the community, and there is a tone of elasticity which promises well for the future.

The General Revenue for the year ended 31st December 1875 amounted to £1,143,312 5s. 10d., to which must be added the balance to credit at the commencement of the year, £92,677 2s. 2d., making a total income of £1,235,989 8s.

The Total Expenditure by the Government during the same period was £1,176,412 18s. 10d., leaving a balance at the end of the twelve months of £59,576 9s. 2d.

The Public Loan Account is kept distinct from that of the General Revenue.

The receipts of the year amounted to five pounds twelve shillings per head of the population. The amount of revenue contributed through the Customs—the only source of general taxation—was thirty-three shillings per head, an amount lower than the rate of taxation in the Mother Country, or in any of the other Australian Colonies.

The following table gives the amount of revenue derived under the several heads of receipt :—

HEADS OF RECEIPT.

	£
Customs	339,103
Marine	9,237
Rents, &c., crown lands	85,744
Rents—ordinary	1,120
Licences—business	13,920
Postages and telegraphs	78,818
Fines, fees, and forfeitures	27,582
Sales of Government property	437
Reimbursements in aid	11,991
Miscellaneous	4,561
Interest and exchange	2,762
Railways and tramways	183,095
Waterworks	30,895
Land sales { Proceeds of	177,530
{ Interest on credit sales	112,038
Immigration	4,473
	£1,143,312

In young communities the general Government has necessarily imposed upon it functions and duties from which, in more advanced conditions of society, the State is exempt. The construction of railways, waterworks, telegraphs, roads, public buildings, &c. must, if entered into at all, be undertaken at the public cost. Moreover, such works must, in common prudence, be constructed on a scale in advance of the actual requirements of the moment. In South Australia such expenditure forms a large proportion of the whole, will benefit future generations equally with the present, and must not be regarded as ordinary current cost of Government.

The subjoined table shows the expenditure, specified under the respective heads of service for which it was incurred :—

HEADS OF EXPENDITURE.

	£
Civil list	18,900
The legislature	10,803
Civil establishments	36,035
Judicial and legal departments	31,059
Police	50,245
Gaols and prisons	12,337
Education	42,636
Charitable institutions	54,012
Military defences	882
Postal and telegraph services	132,744
Customs	11,577
Harbours and lights	16,498
Public works	247,940
Railways and tramways	177,456
Waterworks	18,117
Survey and crown lands	37,466
Retiring allowances, &c.	9,919
Interest and exchange	4,838
Miscellaneous	58,894
Immigration	27,139
Interest on loans for public works	142,476
Redemption of ditto	34,400
	£1,176,412

The payments may be summarised as follows :—The ordinary expenses of Government (including judicial and legal departments, police, gaols, prisons, &c.) amount to £262,000, or twenty-five shillings per head of the population, being eight shillings less than the taxation; £43,000 is devoted to education; £54,000 to charitable institutions; and £328,000 is required for the service of reproductive works. Among these latter, railways require £177,000, the receipts from that source being £183,000. The waterworks take £18,000, and the receipts therefrom are £31,000. The post and telegraph services absorb £132,000, and the revenue contributed by them is £78,000. The interest on the bonded debt amounts to £142,000, averaging fourteen shillings per head of the population; but an amount very much larger than this is annually saved by the reduced cost of carriage and other facilities afforded to the public by the works constructed out of the loans upon which this interest accrues. The cost of the survey and management of Crown lands was last year £37,000; and £27,000 was devoted to the introduction of immigrants.

The expenditure on public works and in reduction of loans amounted to £282,000, being 105,000 more than the sum received during the year from the proceeds of the sales of waste lands. The Crown lands being the capital of the Colony, it is important to note that not only were the receipts derived from their sale devoted intact to improving the public estate, but a sum equal to one-third more, derived from the general revenue, was also expended in the same direction.

LOANS FOR PUBLIC WORKS.

Legislative sanction has been accorded from time to time for the raising of moneys by way of loan for the prosecution of reproductive public works, such as railways, tramways, waterworks, telegraphs, harbour improvements, and other public purposes. The following return shows the amount of Public Debt outstanding on 31st December 1875 for each of the several Public Works, and the total rate of indebtedness per head of the population, and for each undertaking :—

| | Public Debt. | |
	Amount.	Rate per Head.
	£	£ s. d.
Railways	1,381,600	6 11 0
Tramways	131,500	0 12 0
Waterworks	511,600	2 8 6
Telegraphs	378,400	1 16 0
Harbours and lights	328,000	1 12 0
Roads	236,000	1 2 0
Public purposes	168,500	0 16 0
Northern Territory...	185,000	0 17 6
Total	£3,320,600	£15 15 0

If it be asked what the Colony has to show in the shape of permanent improvements, it may be answered that there are three hundred and forty miles of railway. The city, port, and suburbs of Adelaide, with sixty thousand residents, have an abundant and constant water supply. Harbours have been deepened and improved, and navigation rendered easy by an almost perfect system of lighthouses. Eighteen hundred miles of macadamised roads are in effective order, and the Province is traversed from north to south and from east to west by telegraphs, over five thousand miles in length, bringing us into instantaneous communication with the whole world.

The earlier loans were issued bearing six per cent. interest, but those of late years bear four per cent. only. The present price of South Australian four per cents is 95½. Interest and redemption is payable in London on 1st January and 1st July in each year. The currency of the bonds is generally thirty years. Redemptions to the amount of £678,400 have been made since the first issue of bonds in 1854.

BANKING.

Six banking institutions carry on business within the Province, namely, the Bank of South Australia, Bank of Australasia, Union Bank of Australia, National Bank of Australasia, English, Scottish, and Australian Chartered Bank, and Bank of Adelaide, all of which have establishments in the principal seaports and inland townships, numbering altogether sixty-four branches and agencies. Quarterly general abstracts are published of the average amount of liabilities and assets of the several Banks, taken from their weekly statements, and they comprise in each case a return of the notes and bills in circulation, the balances due to other Banks, and deposits with and without interest. The total average liabilities of the six Banks amount to £3,278,121, and the total average assets to £5,157,868. The following table shows the total average assets and liabilities of all the Banks taken for the last quarter of each of the years mentioned :—

	1861.	1866.	1871.	1875.
	£	£	£	£
Liabilities ...	1,021,686	1,715,895	1,802,634	3,278,121
Assets... ...	1,869,008	3,620,062	3,524,412	5,157,868

The annexed statement shows the position of each Bank as set forth in the quarterly return of December 1875 :—

	Bank of South Australia.	Bank of Australasia.	Union Bank.	National Bank.	English, Scottish, and Australian Chartered Bank.	Bank of Adelaide.	Total.
LIABILITIES.	£	£	£	£	£	£	£
Notes in circulation not bearing interest	93,898	32,520	16,913	151,690	65,315	58,964	419,330
Bills in circulation	5,011	2,608	1,772	4,386	—	1,254	15,066
Balances due to other Banks	13,616	—	—	11,884	1,514	54,161	81,176
Deposits	511,522	219,407	186,386	856,471	480,615	478,131	2,762,516
Total average liabilities	654,082	254,536	205,113	1,024,431	547,416	592,511	3,278,121
ASSETS.	£	£	£	£	£	£	£
Coined gold, silver, and other metals	171,658	56,438	49,177	162,251	47,942	82,050	569,522
Gold and silver in bullion or ingots	—	—	—	—	12,051	1,462	13,514
Government securities	—	—	—	25,000	—	—	25,000
Landed property and Bank premises	35,954	15,325	14,714	33,256	11,294	17,724	128,269
Notes and bills of other Banks	5,481	4,372	2,962	14,065	7,115	4,413	38,411
Balances due from other Banks	48,242	—	—	9,701	878	6,918	65,741
Notes and bills discounted and other debts to banks not before enumerated	807,781	370,828	321,139	1,062,911	744,338	1,007,376	4,317,378
Total average assets	1,069,120	146,963	390,991	1,307,191	823,651	1,119,916	5,157,868
Capital stock paid up	500,000	1,200,000	1,250,000	750,000	600,000	400,000	4,700,000
Reserved profits at time of declaring last dividend	175,636	374,119	506,471	255,617	60,000	90,000	1,461,843
Rate of last dividend declared	10 per cent.	12½ per cent.	16 per cent.	12 per cent.	8 per cent.	10 per cent.	—
Original price of shares	£25	£40	£25	£4	£20	£4	—
Present price of shares	£41	£69	£36	£7 5s.	£26	£6 8s. 6d.	—

From the above it appears that the amount of coin, bullion, and Government securities held was eleven per cent. of the assets; and the liabilities amounted to sixty-three per cent. of the assets.

The rate of interest allowed to depositors by the several Banks during the past year varied as follows :—

Interest on fixed deposits, at 30 days' notice, at £3 10s. to £5.
     ,,   ,,   for three months, and at 30 days' notice, £3 10s. to £5.
     ,,   ,,   for six months, £4 to £5.
     ,,   ,,   for twelve months, £4 10s. to £5.
     Special arrangements for particular lodgments.

The course of exchange was as follows :—

On drafts issued during 1875—

On London, at 60 days' sight ... ... 1st quarter, 1 per cent. premium.
     2nd   ,,   1   ,,   ,,
     3rd   ,,   1   ,,   ,,
     4th   ,, $\frac{1}{2}$,,   ,,

On neighbouring Colonies, at sight, 1st quarter, $\frac{1}{4}$, $\frac{1}{2}$, 1 per cent. premium.
     2nd   ,, $\frac{1}{4}$, $\frac{1}{2}$, 1   ,,   ,,
     3rd   ,, $\frac{1}{4}$, $\frac{1}{2}$, 1   ,,   ,,
     4th   ,, $\frac{1}{4}$, $\frac{1}{2}$, 1   ,,   ,,

On private bills purchased during 1875—

On London, at 60 days' sight ... ... 1st quarter, 1 per cent. discount.
     2nd   ,,   1   ,,   ,,
     3rd   ,,   1   ,,   ,,
     4th   ,, $\frac{1}{2}$,,   ,,

On neighbouring Colonies, at sight ... 1st quarter, $\frac{3}{4}$, $\frac{1}{2}$ per cent. discount.
     2nd   ,, $\frac{3}{4}$, $\frac{1}{2}$,,   ,,
     3rd   ,, $\frac{3}{4}$, $\frac{1}{2}$,,   ,,
     4th   ,, $\frac{3}{4}$, $\frac{1}{2}$,,   ,,

The present (1875) rate of discount on local bills is— Under 65 days, 8 per cent. ; 65 to 95 days, 8 per cent. ; 95 to 125 days, 9 to 10 per cent. ; and over 125 days, 10 per cent.

SAVINGS BANKS.

As evidencing the power of accumulation and thrifty habits of the industrial classes, it is only necessary to refer to the progress of one of the most popular of our local institutions— the Savings Bank of South Australia. It was established in 1848, incorporated by Act of Parliament, and is managed by a Board of Trustees appointed by the Governor. In addition to the Head Office, there are agencies established in thirty of the principal townships throughout the Colony, in connection with Telegraph and Money Order Offices. Deposits are received in sums from One Shilling up to £500; but interest is only allowed up to £250. The rate of interest paid is now five pounds per cent. per annum. The following statement shows the operations and progress of the institution, at intervals, and gives a fair index of the position of the working classes who most largely avail themselves of the facilities afforded by the bank for the safe investment of small sums at a fair rate of interest.

Years.	Number of Depositors.	Amount deposited.	Amount withdrawn.	Amount of Depositors' Balances.	Total Funds.
		£	£	£	£
1848 ...	214	6,473	1,180	5,313	5,414
1851 ...	732	15,224	12 761	14,340	14,785
1856 ...	1,469	29,328	27,142	52,775	57,060
1861 ...	3,248	65,373	37,627	121,414	131,590
1866 ...	7,679	124,427	147,524	249,329	266,700
1871 ...	14,270	237,053	191,161	490,844	516,999
1875 ...	22,662	419,914	393,686	816,827	845,276

The total number of depositors last year was 22,662, the average sum at the credit of each being thirty-six pounds. The total deposits of the year amounted to £420,000, and the total funds of the institution to £845,276, invested chiefly in Government securities (£291,334) and on mortgage of freehold property (£239,711). The Reserve Fund amounts to £28,448. In South Australia, the depositors in Savings Banks are one in ten of the population, in New South Wales one in twenty, and in Victoria one in thirty.

LAND AND ITS OCCUPATION.

Excluding that portion of the Province known as the Northern Territory, the total area of South Australia is about 383,328 square miles, or 245,329,920 acres. It may be roughly estimated that not more than 250,000 square miles are at present put to profitable use. Agricultural settlement has not extended 150 miles from the coast, and pastoral occupation may be said to have reached no farther than 500 miles, although squatters have lately taken up large areas of land discovered by recent explorations (lying chiefly on the route of the overland telegraph), and which are considered capable of carrying stock. Twenty-six counties have been proclaimed up to date, embracing 40,967 square miles, or 26,218,880 acres. Of this large area, only 6,283,881 acres have been alienated from the Crown, amounting, nevertheless, to thirty acres for every man, woman, and child in the Colony, or one hundred and twenty acres for each male adult. About one in every five acres of the alienated land is under tillage; the remainder is used for pastoral purposes only. All land is surveyed by the Government prior to sale, and is divided into farms of extent varying from eighty to six hundred and forty acres, the necessary reserves being made for railways, public highways, watering of stock, &c. This land is thrown open for selection in large quantities, from 50,000 to 100,000 acres being put up at one time. At present there is as much as half a million of acres of land surveyed and open for immediate selection. The total area of land held for pastoral purposes beyond the boundaries of the counties mentioned is estimated to be 188,000 square miles.

The table on page 45 shows the names of counties, their area, the quantity of land sold, and the acreage surveyed and open for selection.

At the close of 1875, of the total area of land alienated from the Crown, namely 6,283,881 acres, 4,634,549 acres had been purchased in fee simple for cash, and 1,649,332 acres under the system of deferred payments. The demand for land during the past twelvemonths was very great, being more considerable than in any previous year, amounting to 686,050 acres, as compared with 424,130 acres in 1874. Of this quantity, 130,079 acres have been sold for cash, realizing £175,067; 555,971 acres were taken up by selectors who agreed to pay on the expiry of their term of credit £764,140, paying a deposit of £76,423, which is treated as interest during the term of agreement. With regard to the 130,079 acres of land sold for cash during the year, which, as has been stated, realized £175,067, it will be understood that 351 acres were town lands, averaging £33 an acre, or £13 per acre more than the price realized for town lands in the previous year; that 6,701 acres were suburban lands which realized an average price of £2 17s. per acre, and the remainder was country land, the average price of which (where the land—namely, 28,337 acres—was sold outright at a fixed price) was £1 0s. 1½d., or

Counties.		Area in Square Miles.	Area in Acres.	Purchased Land to 31st December 1875.	Extent of Land held by Freeholders.	Land open for Selection.
				Acres.		Acres.
Adelaide	... ...	1,161	743,040	594,369	313,010	1,220
Gawler	... ...	979	626,560	438,667	220,731	27,652
Light	... ...	848	542,720	518,183	372,598	198
Stanley	... ...	1,420	908,800	773,300	433,863	29,873
Victoria	... ...	1,527	977,280	603,793	178,464	5,128
Kimberley	... ...	1,440	921,600	39,793	1,737	9,414
Dalhousie	... ...	1,220	780,800	206,789	41,061	22,845
Fergusson	... ...	2,000	1,280,000	304,424	147,142	77,635
Daly	... ...	1,236	791,040	283,684	62,016	68,112
Froine	... ...	1,404	898,560	269,384	19,481	39,363
Hindmarsh	... ...	1,032	660,480	340,788	207,311	38,362
Sturt	... ...	1,343	859,520	337,443	212,209	87,653
Eyre	... ...	1,340	857,600	245,403	138,203	61,796
Burra	... ...	1,767	1,130,880	217,473	151,950	2,279
Young	... ...	2,015	1,289,600	690	320	—
Hamley	... ...	2,135	1,366,400	80	80	—
Alfred	... ...	1,855	1,187,200	—	—	—
Albert	... ...	2,136	1,367,040	1,765	1,735	—
Russell	... ...	1,542	986,880	157,498	86,097	16,693
Buckingham	... ...	1,612	1,031,680	34,616	2,198	829
Cardwell	... ...	1,856	1,187,840	1,234	794	—
MacDonnell	... ...	1,944	1,244,160	119,835	52,824	15,165
Robe	... ...	2,028	1,297,920	236,922	239,552	9,286
Grey	... ...	2,347	1,502,080	453,418	368,221	11,352
Flinders	... ...	1,100	704,000	100,979	67,663	44,873
Carnarvon	... ...	1,680	1,075,200	2,884	4,062	—
Total	...	40,967	26,218,880	6,283,414	3,323,322	569,728
Pastoral Districts	...	—	—	2,238	352	—
Grand Total	...	40,967	26,218,880	6,285,652	3,323,674	569,728

1½d. per acre above the upset price of one pound. 86,784 of the acres which have been sold on credit, and the purchase of which is now completed, realized £1 4s. 7d. an acre, or 4s. 7d. above the upset price of one pound.

Turning to the sales of Crown lands on credit during the year 1875, and which have been stated as amounting to

555,971 acres, 516,640 acres were selected by agriculturists who entered into an agreement to reside upon the land either personally or by a servant, and to carry out the necessary conditions of improvement and cultivation, agreeing to pay on the average £1 7s. 6d. per acre at the termination of their agreement, when they would become entitled to the fee simple of the land. Selections which had been taken up previously, and had been forfeited either voluntarily or by reason of neglect in carrying out the requirements of the Act, were re-selected to the extent of 25,387 acres, and the average price agreed to be paid by the new holders was £1 10s. 8d. per acre.

The following table shows the number of acres sold on credit since the introduction of the existing land system and the aggregate amount to be paid on the termination of the agreements :—

	Area in Acres.	Amount.
1871	289,892	£372,536
1872	299,957	397,284
1873	279,512	435,485
1874	352,166	596 096
1875	555,971	764,140
Total ...	1,777,498	£2,565,544

The total quantity of land taken up during the five years since the Act has been in operation is 1,777,498 acres, for which £2,565,544 was agreed to be paid. Of this amount, £2,406,251 still remains on credit awaiting the termination of the agreements.

The following are the principal provisions of the Land Act of 1872 :—" All waste lands, other than township and suburban, have a fixed value put upon them by the Commissioner of Crown Lands, not less than £1 per acre. In improved or reclaimed lands the cost per acre of the improvements and reclamation is added to the upset price of £1 per acre. Those lands which have been open for selection, or which have been offered at auction, and neither selected nor sold, may at the end of five years be offered for sale in blocks of not more than 3000 acres, on lease for ten years, at an annual rental of not less than 6d. per acre, with a right of purchase at any time during the currency of the lease at £1 per acre.

"When any lands are declared open for selection, by proclamation in the *Government Gazette*, at a fixed price, a day is appointed for receiving applications for sections, not to exceed in the aggregate 640 acres, or one square mile. The person making the application shall pay at the time a deposit of ten per cent. on the fixed price, which sum shall be taken as payment of three years' interest in advance upon the purchase money. If the price of the land is £100, the selector would have to pay a deposit of £10, which will be all he will be required to pay the Government for three years—about three and three-quarters per cent. per annum. At the end of three years he will have to pay another ten per cent., which will also be received as interest for the next three years. If at the end of six years he is not prepared to pay the whole of the purchase money, he can obtain other four years' credit on payment of half the purchase money, and interest in advance on the other half, at the rate of four per cent. per annum. Lands which have been open for selection two years, and not taken up, may be purchased for cash. The scrub lands may also be taken up on very favourable terms, on long leases.

"A credit selector may reside on his land either personally or by substitute. The personal resident, however, has advantages which he who resides by deputy has not. In cases of simultaneous applications for the same block, the personal resident has the preference over the other; and at the end of five years, the selector who has resided on the land and made all the required improvements and complied with all the conditions may, by paying his purchase money, obtain the fee simple of his selection. The selector who occupies by substitute cannot get the freehold until the end of six years.

"Purchasers upon credit will be required to reside, either personally or by deputy, upon the land at least nine months in the year; and absence for any longer time than three months in one year renders the agreement liable to forfeiture.

"The credit purchaser will be required to make substantial improvements upon the land before the end of the second year, to the extent of 5s. per acre; before the end of the third year, 7s. 6d. per acre; before the end of the fourth year,

10s. per acre. 'Such improvements to consist of all or any
of the following, that is to say :—Erecting a dwelling-house
or farm building, sinking wells, constructing water tanks or
reservoirs, putting up fencing, draining, or clearing or grubbing
the said land.' The fences must be of a substantial character.

"The credit purchaser is required, during each year until
the purchase money is paid off, to plough and have under
cultivation at least one-fifth of the land; but in the event of
his not cultivating this quantity during the first year, he will
be required to cultivate two-fifths during the second year."

The diagram A (opposite) shows at a glance the progress
made in settlement and agriculture during the last twenty-five
years.

AGRICULTURE.

Where over four-tenths of the male population of a
community are engaged in farming pursuits, the necessity for
collecting authentic information regarding the progress of
agriculture is sufficiently apparent. For many years past the
annual statistics collected on this subject have afforded a mass
of records the value of which every year becomes greater.

The Special Commissioner of the Crown Colonies at the
Vienna Exhibition (Mr. William Robinson, now Governor of
the Bahamas), in reporting to the Imperial Government,
said :—" Of all the British Colonies, South Australia exhibits
the most striking picture at present of farming industry, and
on the whole seems to be the place where, good as the
labourer's condition may be elsewhere, he has, by prudence
and industry, the best chance of rising in the social scale, and
becoming in his turn the employer of labour," and further,
" the yeomanry who have found a home in South Australia,
and who are at once tillers of the soil and employers of labour,
are more than any one class the real bone and sinew of the
Colony; and the industry which has so widely covered the
land with farms, homesteads, tillage, and fencing of every
description, has probably never been equalled in its result in
any British Colony in the same number of years by the same
amount of population. It is by the spread of agriculture that

A.

ADELAIDE, SOUTH AUSTRALIA.

DIAGRAM SHOWING THE POPULATION, ACRES SOLD, ACRES CULTIVATED, ACRES IN WHEAT, AND WHEAT HARVESTED.

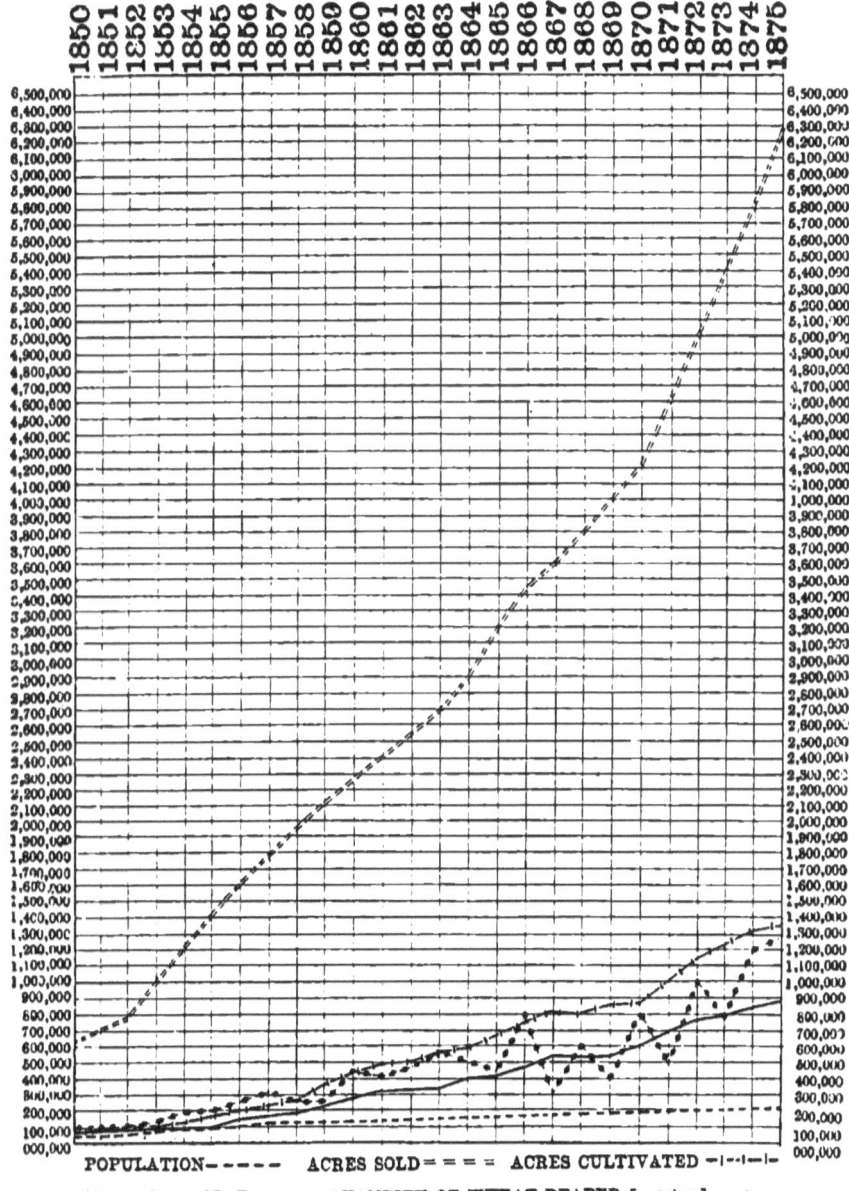

POPULATION- - - - -   ACRES SOLD = = = =   ACRES CULTIVATED -|--|-|-

ACRES IN WHEAT———   QUANTITY OF WHEAT REAPED [quarters] → + +

the greatest amount of industrial prosperity has been created, and the real settlement of the country most effectually accomplished." An analysis of the statistics of the last fifteen years abundantly proves the soundness of His Excellency's judgment. The area of land alienated in South Australia is 6,283,881 acres, or 120 acres for each male adult. Of this area, 1,330,484 acres are under cultivation, showing a result of one in every 4·3 acres of purchased land to be under tillage. There are six acres and a half of cultivated land for each individual of the population, equal to twenty-eight acres for each adult male, or sixty acres for each person returned at the last census as engaged on farms. The following table exhibits very clearly the operation of the new land system, as regards settlement and cultivation, since its inauguration in 1871 :—

Counties.	Acres under Cultivation.				
	1870-71.	1871-2.	1872-3.	1873-4.	1874-5.
Adelaide	181,360	177,808	171,615	169,378	165,350
Gawler	159,755	179,192	197,193	193,002	199,158
Light	248,400	262,526	264,624	251,951	245,491
Stanley	125,421	155,580	167,502	162,160	167,715
Victoria	5,697	20,263	79,539	116,981	154,494
Kimberley	—	—	931	2,054	7,760
Dalhousie	—	—	1,894	8,569	29,497
Fergusson	1,412	6,796	10,731	25,789	38,744
Daly	15,335	24,869	43,231	43,156	68,246
Frome	764	542	507	6,247	16,268
Hindmarsh	77,585	73,911	63,926	61,153	54,942
Sturt	40,107	34,221	37,782	43,679	35,767
Eyre	27,648	27,937	37,585	37,853	45,790
Burra	11,445	18,103	19,865	23,981	24,943
Hamley	2	6	5	16	14
Albert	—	1	—	—	—
Russell	7,946	9,234	11,503	12,686	13,591
Buckingham	99	94	463	1,682	2,763
Cardwell	262	229	150	131	290
MacDonnell	2,922	4,163	5,535	5,767	4,936
Robe	5,924	6,922	7,676	8,537	8,573
Grey	41,158	36,548	36,612	44,684	40,313
Flinders	4,240	4,427	4,612	4,637	4,903
Carnarvon	1,045	1,056	993	759	772
Pastoral Districts	479	228	372	221	164
Total	959,006	1,044,656	1,164,846	1,225,073	1,330,484

About two-thirds of the total area cultivated is cropped with wheat, of which cereal 839,638 acres were reaped last year, yielding an aggregate of 9,862,693 bushels, the largest quantity yet produced in the Colony. The crop was a fair average one, of excellent quality, and, considering the scarcity of farm labour, was safely and early secured. It is important to note that, whilst the area of wheat grown has increased more than one hundred per cent. during the last ten years, the population has only increased thirty per cent.

The harvest now being gathered is expected to produce twelve million bushels, which will permit of an export of over 230,000 tons of breadstuffs, after providing for home requirements.

Annexed is a statement showing the total area of land under cultivation, the acreage under wheat, the gross produce of the harvest, and the average yield per acre at intervals of five years :—

Seasons.	Acres Cultivated.	Acres under Wheat.	Produce, Wheat.	Average per Acre.	
			Bushels.	Bush.	lbs.
1860-61	428,816	273,672	3,576,593	13	4
1865-6	660,569	410,608	3,587,800	8	44
1870-71	959,006	604,761	6,961,164	11	30
1874-5	1,330,484	839,638	9,862,693	11	45

With regard to the comparatively low average yield above shown, it must be borne in mind, in judging of the relative productiveness of the soil of South Australia as compared with that of other countries, that a great portion of the land has been sown with wheat continuously for many successive years without manure or rest, and, being in the hands of small proprietors, has received only the minimum of cultivation. This, of course, tends to reduce the general average; but there are many districts where farming is carried on on a large scale, and with proper appliances, where the yield of this cereal is from ten to fifteen bushels per acre beyond the average shown above.

As evidence of the high quality of the South Australian grain, it may be mentioned that the prize wheat exhibited at the Agricultural Shows during the past ten years has averaged 68 lbs. weight to the Imperial bushel.

In 1865-6 there were 423,881 acres under grain, viz. wheat,

barley, oats, and peas, and in 1874-5 there were 860,475 acres ; so that within the period specified the acreage so occupied was more than doubled.

Under other crops, flax, hay, potatoes, orchard, garden, vineyard, and fallow land, there were 229,182 acres in 1865-6, and 442,933 in 1874-5, or nearly double. The total quantity under cultivation at the earlier date was 660,569, and at the later, 1,330,484, or more than double the acreage. The extent of land now under hay cultivation is 160,931, and of fallow-land, 264,327 acres. In 1858, only eighteen years after the Province was founded, there were 89,945 acres of land under wheat culture ; in 1865-6, there were 410,608 ; and in 1874-5, no less than 839,638 acres.

The following table shows the extent of land under cultivation, and each description of crop, at quinquennial intervals since 1860-61 :—

Crops.	Acres under Cultivation in Years			
	1860-61.	1865-6.	1870-71.	1874-5.
For Grain—				
Wheat	273,672	410,608	604,761	*839,638
Barley	11,336	9,362	22,912	13,724
Oats	2,273	2,872	6,188	2,785
Pens	—	969	3,719	4,328
For Green Forage—				
Wheat, Barley, Oats, &c.	2,174	2,514	2,600	1,117
Sorghum	116	230	—	—
Lucerne	1,726	1,424	3,445	6,699
Permanent Artificial Grasses	1,836	3,408	3,712	19,260
Flax	—	—	186	274
Other Crops	584	1,272	829	434
Hay	55,818	101,996	140,316	160,931
Potatoes	2,348	2,775	3,376	4,582
Orchard	2,147	2,554	2,763	3,077
Garden	3,910	3,919	4,345	4,257
Vineyard	3,180	6,629	6,131	5,051
Fallow Land	67,696	110,037	153,723	264,327
Totals	428,816	660,569	959,006	1,330,484

Vine culture is an important and progressive industry. There are 5050 acres of land devoted to this purpose, the total number of vines being 5,155,988, of which 4,874,507 are in bearing. The produce of these vineyards for the year ended March 1875 was 648,186 gallons of wine, about one hundred and thirty gallons per acre.

The suitability of the soil and climate of South Australia to the growth of wine was soon discovered by the early settlers, some of whom had brought from Europe a variety of high class vine cuttings. The slopes of the hills produce wines of a full-bodied character similar to those of Spain and Portugal, whilst those made in the more elevated districts resemble the lighter wines of the Rhine. Whilst the local demand is fully supplied at very cheap rates, a considerable export trade in wines of a higher character is carried on, and which might be increased to a great extent but for obstructive fiscal laws. Whilst the lower class wines of the Continent are admitted to the ports of the Mother Country at a minimum rate of duty, the Customs dues charged upon superior wines from Australia are so high as to be almost prohibitory.

That the wines of South Australia are, as a rule, of a high character is proved by the fact that they have always been awarded prizes at the several Great International Exhibitions.

The introduction of flax-growing into the ordinary routine of farm operations, has been followed by considerable success. The prices realized for this commodity in the European markets have been very encouraging.

Considerable attention has also been paid to the manufacture of preserved fruits, and the drying of raisins and currants. This branch of industry is rapidly progressing, and, whilst it now goes far to supply local requirements, will probably soon develop into an export trade.

Almond trees are of rapid growth, and large quantities of a superior description of soft-shell almond are gathered yearly for home consumption and for shipment.

South Australia possesses all the conditions requisite for the successful and profitable culture of the olive. This tree, like the vine, was early introduced into the Colony, and its growth and productiveness have been so remarkable that large planta-tions have been established and stocked with the best Continental varieties. Olive oil of the most delicate character has been expressed, and gained awards at the various Exhibitions. Its purity and general superiority over the imported article of commerce has acquired for it a first position in the market. The produce of the plantations is eagerly purchased by persons who have entered upon the business of the manufacture of oil. It may be stated, as showing the importance which is attached to the cultivation of the olive, as of the mulberry (of which several plantations of the most suitable kinds exist for the development of sericulture), the almond, vine, orange, fig, and hop, that the land laws provide that the planting and cultivation of one acre of land with any of these trees shall be equivalent to the cultivation of six acres of cereals.

Orchards, gardens, and vineyards abound, and, in short, the variety and excellence of the fruits and vegetables produced in the Colony cannot be surpassed. The climate and soil enables the productions of temperate and tropical regions to be cultivated almost side by side, and throughout the year; and offers an unlimited field of profitable occupation in connection with ordinary farming pursuits.

PASTORAL OCCUPATION.

Notwithstanding the large area of land lately alienated from the Crown, and the extension of agricultural operations, the acreage of land taken up for squatting purposes and the increase in the number of flocks and herds have been very considerable. All descriptions of stock, whether horses, cattle, or sheep, have thriven and increased rapidly.

Of late years the enclosure and sub-division of runs (enabling the sheep to roam at will during the whole year) has been found to produce greatly improved results, both as regards the quality of the stock and of the wool. Large numbers of sheep are owned by settlers, who advantageously combine sheep-farming with agriculture.

Some conception of the growth of the pastoral interest may be formed from the fact that, whilst in 1851 the total area of land leased from the Crown for pastoral purposes was 15,000 square miles, at the present time there are no less than 200,000 square miles in occupation. During the same period the number of horses has increased from 6500 to 93,000; of horned cattle from 75,000 to 185,000; and of sheep from 1,000,000 to over 6,000,000, whilst the exports of wool have increased from 4000 to 118,000 bales.

The following table shows the progressive increase in horses, cattle, and sheep, at each quinquennial period between 1856 and 1875 :—

Years.	Horses.	Cattle.	Sheep.
1856	22,260	272,746	1,962,460
1861	52,597	265,434	3,038,356
1866	70,829	123,820	3,911,610
1871	78,125	143,463	4,412,055
1875	93,122	185,342	6,120,211

With reference to the slight comparative increase in cattle it should be noted that more profitable results are found to accrue from the breeding of sheep than from great cattle. The latter pursuit is more extensively followed in the neighbouring colonies.

During the last ten years the average price of first-class fat bullocks has averaged £14 10s., and of first-class fat wethers, 15s. per head.

The enclosure of the sheep runs, the formation of dams and reservoirs in which large bodies of water can be stored, and the sinking of wells, are the most important improvements required, and are those to which the greatest attention is now being paid. By these means an immense area of land has been opened up, and stocked with both sheep and cattle.

Almost limitless tracts of country bordering on the trans-continental telegraph line, as well as land laid open by recent explorations, are awaiting pastoral occupation.

MANUFACTURES.

A few years ago, flour mills and tanneries were almost the only representatives of local manufactures; whilst these have largely increased in number and efficiency, many important additions have been made to the list. The following is a statement of the more important; some are conducted on an extensive scale, and, from the constantly increasing number of hands employed, manufacturing industry generally would appear to be in a highly flourishing state. It will be noticed that most of the industries mentioned have their raw material at hand in the produce of the country, and are for that reason much more likely to be permanent in their character.

Milling is a very important branch of trade, over seventy-five thousand tons of flour having been exported during the past year. There are eighty-five steam flour mills in the Province, with 1500 horse-power, driving 275 pairs of stones.

Four meat-preserving establishments are in operation, and there are eight boiling-down works.

Sixty tanneries and fellmongeries, and several large wool-washing works, are distributed throughout the country; ten soap and candle factories; five bone-dust mills; and two glue and size works.

Thirty-one steam saw mills, twenty-seven foundries, eighty-six agricultural implement works (chiefly for reaping and winnowing machines), and twenty-nine coach and waggon builders' shops are in active work. ·

In addition to five patent slips, there are eight ship and twelve boat building yards.

Several marble and sixteen slate quarries of excellent quality, and over one hundred building-stone quarries, have been opened, of which latter nineteen are free-stone, a superior description being largely used in public and private buildings. There are seventy brickyards in operation (including six for fire-bricks), sixty limekilns, and seven potteries and tile and pipe works.

The gasworks of the Colony are eight in number, of which two are for the supply of the City of Adelaide and suburbs, one is at Port Adelaide, and the remaining five are in the principal country towns.

Besides one woollen tweed factory, there are six clothing factories, four hat factories, twelve boot and shoe factories, and four dye works. There are also three flax mills, three rope walks, and two brush manufactories at work.

There are twenty-nine breweries; thirty soda-water and cordial factories; one hundred and two wine-making establishments; ten biscuit bakeries; ten jam and preserve and seven confectionery manufactories; six dried fruit and three olive-oil factories, and one ice-work.

Among other miscellaneous local productions and manufactures, are the following:—Barilla, billiard table, baking powder, blacking, cayenne pepper, cement, cigars, fibre, glass bottles, plaster of Paris, washing machines, sauces and pickles, salt, safety fuze, gas stoves, iron safes, bedsteads, galvanized iron and tin ware.

IMPORT AND EXPORT TRADE.

The expansion of commerce and the development of the material resources of South Australia are clearly exhibited in the returns under the above head. Although able, as large agricultural and pastoral producers, to supply ourselves with the greater portion of the necessaries of life, we are dependent upon Great Britain and foreign markets for a considerable number of articles which enter into general consumption.

The total value of the imports and exports to and from each country, exhibiting the balance of trade, is shown in the subjoined table. The combined import and export trade of 1875 amounted to £9,000,000 sterling, of which £4,200,000 were imports, and £4,800,000 exports, showing a balance in favour of South Australia of £600,000. The total external trade averaged £45 per head of the population, or £175 for each adult male. The imports amounted to £20 per head of the population, and the exports to £24; or, taking the adult male population as the basis of the calculation, the imports amounted to £80, and the exports to £96, or an excess of exports over imports of £16 per adult male.

Countries.	Imports.	Exports.	Excess of Imports.	Excess of Exports.
	£	£	£	£
Great Britain	2,381,673	2,612,817	—	231,143
Victoria	822,660	852,715	—	30,054
New South Wales ...	477,147	689.115	—	211,967
Western Australia	36,347	62.372	—	26,025
New Zealand	9,406	44,115	—	34,709
Queensland	22,888	216,800	—	193,912
Tasmania	40,272	2,794	37,478	—
India	36,969	30,679	6,289	—
Ceylon	3,972	4.187	—	215
Cape Colony	1,133	137,018	—	135,885
Natal	5,653	44,445	—	38,792
Mauritius	95,743	38,732	57,011	—
Singapore	5.226	241	4,984	—
Hong Kong	28,379	40	28,339	—
Canada	21.687	—	21,687	—
United States	28,502	—	28,502	—
New Caledonia	81	46,315	—	46,234
China	82,933	9	82.924	—
Sweden and Norway ...	63,068	—	63,068	—
Java	40,061	19,583	20,477	—
Brazil	—	3,000	—	3,000
France	—	70	—	70
Total	£4,203,802	£4,805,051	£350,761	£952,010

Of the total imports, £4,203,802 in value, more than one-half, viz. £2,381,673, came from the United Kingdom, £882,660 from Victoria, £477,147 from New South Wales, £214,645 from Foreign States, and the remainder from various British possessions.

Of the total exports, £4,805,051 value, products representing £2,612,817 were exported to the Mother Country, £852,715 to Victoria, £689,115 to New South Wales, £68,977 to Foreign States, and the remainder to other British possessions.

The following table shows the total imports and exports for the years stated :—

IMPORT AND EXPORT TRADE.

Years.	Total.	Imports.	Exports.
	£	£	£
1851	1,292,864	690,777	602,087
1856	3,032,269	1,366,529	1,665,740
1861	4,008,329	1,976,018	2,032,311
1866	5,693,879	2,835,142	2,858,737
1871	5,740,419	2,158,022	3,582,397
1875	9,008,853	4,203,802	4,805,051

Since 1851, the commerce of the Colony has increased seven-fold, from £1,292,864 to £9,008,853 sterling. This is clearly shown in Diagram B (page 60). The last five years have shown a rapid expansion, trade having increased from £5,740,419 to £9,008,853, or by sixty per cent.

The following table shows for each of the past ten years the total import and export trade, the total imports showing the home consumption and re-exportations; also, the total exports, distinguishing those of the produce of the Colony, and showing the balances of produce exported over imports consumed :—

Years.	Combined Import and Export Trade.	Total Imports.	Imports retained for Home Consumption.	Imports re-exported.	Total Exports.	Exports of Produce of the Colony.	Balance Produce exported over Imports consumed.
	£	£	£	£	£	£	£
1866	5,693,879	2,835,142	2,516,128	319,014	2,858,737	2,539,723	23,595
1867	5,671,016	2,506,394	2,117,867	388,527	3,164,622	2,776,095	658,228
1868	5,057,810	2,238,510	2,023,036	215,474	2,819,300	2,603,826	580,796
1869	5,747,805	2,754,770	2,484,174	270,596	2,993,035	2,722,438	238,264
1870	4,449,291	2,029,793	1,733,603	296,190	2,419,488	2,123,297	389,694
1871	5,740,420	2,158,022	1,869,368	292,536	3,582,397	3,289,861	1,521,493
1872	6,510,194	2,801,571	2,587,233	214,536	3,738,623	3,524,087	936,854
1873	8,428,960	3,841,101	3,527,163	302,667	4,587,859	4,285,192	758,029
1874	8,386,145	3,983,290	3,438,874	534,580	4,402,855	3,868,275	429,401
1875	9,008,853	4,203,802	3,840,851	362,951	4,805,051	4,442,100	601,219

In order further to illustrate the description of our external trade, the following statements are appended, showing respectively the quantities or values of the chief articles imported and exported in the five years ending with 1874 :—

IMPORTS—CHIEF ARTICLES, 1870-1874.

	1874.	1873.	1872.	1871.	1870.
Apparel and slops, value (£)	19,383	20,951	2,832	1,246	6,452
Bags and sacks—Cornbags, bales	8,256	11,900	3,407	5,064	3,822
Woolpacks, do.	3,358	3,216	1,886	1,818	1,135
Beer, porter, ale, cider and perry, galls.	215,211	283,375	218,455	174,295	191,114
Blasting-powder, lbs.	179,676	345,252	418,120	156,720	145,750
Boots and shoes, value (£)	60,010	73,422	62,018	48,441	53,496
Candles, lbs.	807,497	618,189	461,900	416,339	471,589
Chicory, lbs.	106,281	191,072	73,926	55,886	107,532
Coals, coke, and other fuel, tons	88,756	83,583	82,502	73,983	52,310
Cocoa and chocolate, lbs.	84,196	90,911	59,337	52,089	56,402
Coffee, lbs.	413,896	371,770	346,234	380,060	549,167
Cutlery and hardware, value (£)	33,579	30,447	21,734	14,011	38,617
Drapery do.	863,865	917,455	647,062	467,697	499,046
Earthenware and china do.	25,979	21,807	10,429	7,764	11,493
Fruit (dried), cwt.	13,243	15,167	9,019	11,110	8,267
Groceries and oilmen's stores, value (£)	48,231	53,902	26,834	26,805	30,154
Hops, lbs.	227,953	274,770	246,853	238,790	310,558
Iron—Bar and rod, tons	3,601	2,778	3,964	2,457	1,954
Sheet and hoop, do.	1,137	1,289	713	667	1,460
Pig, do.	749	512	331	144	686
Manufactures, value (£)	212,489	232,091	95,811	98,183	70,254

B.

ADELAIDE, SOUTH AUSTRALIA.

DIAGRAM SHOWING THE POPULATION, SHIPPING, EXPORTS, IMPORTS, AND COMBINED IMPORT AND EXPORT TRADE.

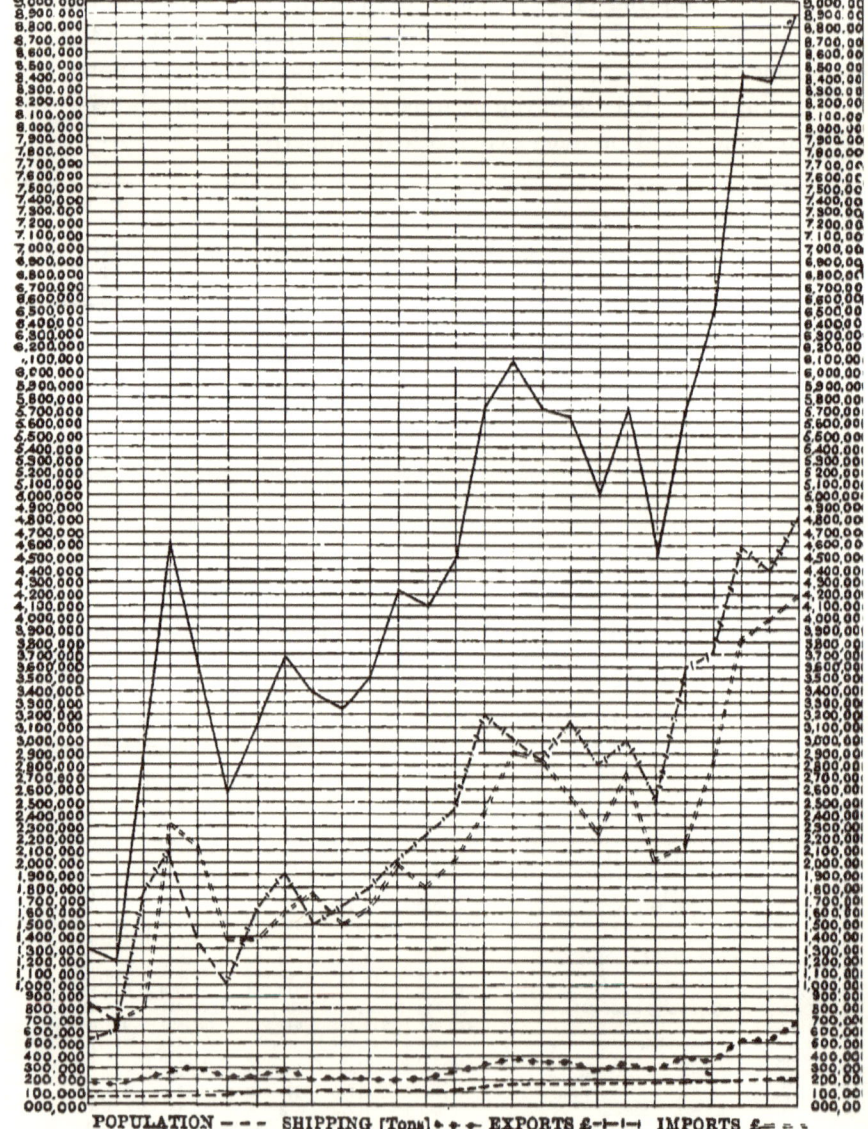

POPULATION - - -   SHIPPING [Tons] + + +   EXPORTS £ +‒+‒+   IMPORTS £ = = =

COMBINED IMPORT AND EXPORT TRADE £ ———

IMPORTS—CHIEF ARTICLES, 1870-1874 (continued).

	1874.	1873.	1872.	1871.	1870.
Implements and tools, value (£)	40,130	36,719	23,180	29,128	17,403
Jewellery, plate, and plated goods, do. ...	39,177	30,670	21,425	15,624	11,367
Malt, centals...	28,341	36,392	22,585	29,773	24,615
Oil—Sperm and other fish oils, gallons ...	6,883	12,698	6,116	12,692	8,693
Linseed, rape, hemp, &c., do. ...	89,173	79,516	72,742	54,966	33,234
Mineral and other oils, do. ...	332,230	237,137	210,322	222,456	167,460
Potatoes, tons	1,413	5,022	2,591	4,774	4,717
Rice, do....	294	488	310	257	260
Saddlery and harness, value (£)	20,406	19,223	16,951	11,385	7,804
Sewing machines, do.	16,205	18,186	12,998	—	—
Spirits—Brandy, gallons	116,013	83,215	87,148	54,787	32,990
Rum, do.	42,841	25,804	29,638	27,128	29,634
Gin, do.	18,558	21,404	13,560	15,283	16,245
Whisky, do.	24,407	26,596	11,615	12,403	13,416
Sugar, cwt.	159,277	141,262	135,227	116,556	59,501
Tea, lbs.	1,699,708	1,678,325	1,025,667	1,221,848	854,887
Tin—Block, value (£)	15,279	25,433	14,895	8,037	5,628
Tobacco, lbs.	400,623	379,507	277,454	241,820	331,012
Cigars, do.	21,129	23,275	14,944	13,748	18,715
Wine, gallons...	45,956	34,881	31,616	22,966	17,611
Wood—Palings, No.	1,566,327	1,687,764	1,098,914	840,635	461,315
Sawn, hewn, &c., loads ...	22,504	29,970	16,450	11,889	15,976

EXPORTS—CHIEF ARTICLES, 1870-1874.

	1874.	1873.	1872.	1871.	1870.
Animals—Horses, No.	42	74	80	162	273
Sheep, do.	1,385	1,049	1,017	430	62
Bacon and Hams, cwt.	35	30	143	29	10
Bark, tons	2,650	4,580	7,850	5,073	5,431
Bones, do.	195	210	880	217	520
Beer, galls.	37,710	20,564	21,257	23,746	21,930
Biscuits, cwt.	862	1,084	496	335	233
Butter and cheese, cwt.	1,206	615	1,564	565	202
Corn—Flour, tons	58,635	57,171	38,319	46,841	27,371
Barley, bushels	6,678	3,658	20,804	28,152	19,672
Bran and pollard, tons ...	2,461	1,477	2,220	3,816	2,167
Wheat, bushels	1,538,464	3,837,616	1,261,424	2,520,432	376,632
Drapery, value (£)	33,839	29,890	26,605	19,687	31,320
Eggs, do.	7,987	8,158	7,965	8,701	8,406
Fish (dried), cwt.	701	277	509	676	823
Fruit (fresh), value (£)	3,764	3,329	3,385	2,292	2,970
Dried, cwt.	610	1,500	1,590	1,325	822
Groceries, value (£)	1,199	2,962	6,439	9,832	9,575
Gum, cwt.	995	476	851	555	5,415
Hay, tons	198	162	663	297	258
Hides and skins, value (£)	16,139	10,593	13,472	8,798	4,266
Honey, cwt.	4	201	34	131	46
Hops, lbs.	21,105	—	—	—	—
Jam, value (£)	3,216	5,969	5,570	4,176	7,396
Leather, cwt.	958	1,329	3,327	4,508	2,884
Metal—Copper, do.	132,587	141,744	149,050	127,911	109,211
Ore—Copper, tons	22,854	27,382	26,964	20,127	20,886
Preserved meats, cwt.	11,248	13,943	12,526	10,000	4,885
Salt, tons	80	184	277	70	214
Soap, cwt.	1,533	—	—	—	—
Sugar, do.	917	4,162	15,126	5,015	1,790
Tallow, do.	25,670	40,106	33,700	63,328	30,142
Tea, lbs.	21,238	46,648	135,038	69,597	123,798
Tobacco, lbs.	40,509	30,518	42,820	57,752	77,631
Wax, cwt.	50	173	41	126	51
Wool, do.	39,844,624	35,973,434	34,650,631	32,656,427	26,218,244
Wine—South Australian, gallons ...	59,174	46,400	41,910	21,788	50,085
Foreign, do. ...	5,586	543	2,768	3,101	3,394
Spirits—Brandy, do. ...	10,657	8,140	9,913	7,590	15,649
Gin, do. ...	1,644	331	539	381	1,212
Rum, do. ...	2,305	2,023	2,429	1,826	4,950
Whisky, do. ...	1,537	970	682	732	960

STAPLE PRODUCTS.

It will be necessary, however, to refer more particularly to the chief sources of the material wealth of the country, which may be classified under the heads of agricultural, pastoral, and mining produce. The following abstract shows the progress made in the exports of staple products from 1851 to the present time, stated at intervals of five years :—

STAPLE PRODUCE EXPORTS.

Years.	Total.	Breadstuffs.	Wool.	Minerals.
	£	£	£	£
1851	540,962	73,359	148,036	310,916.
1856	1,398,867	556,371	412,163	408,042
1861	1,838,639	712,789	623,007	452,172
1866	2,539,723	645,401	990,173	824,501
1871	3,289,861	1,253,429	1,170,885	648,569
1875	4,442,100	1,680,996	1,833,519	762,386

From the foregoing statement, it appears that out of £4,442,100 worth of staple produce, the value of breadstuffs amounted to £1,680,996, or thirty-six per cent. of the whole; that wool represented £1,833,519, or forty-two per cent.; and copper £762,386, or twenty-eight per cent.; the balance of £165,199, or four per cent., being miscellaneous products.

BREADSTUFFS.—The exports of wheat, flour, and other breadstuffs, constitute thirty-six per cent. of the total exports of South Australian produce, and have increased from a total value of £73,000 in 1851 to £1,680,000 in 1875. The exports of breadstuffs during the last twelve months were as follows :— Flour, 76,209 tons, value £819,395; wheat, 479,882 quarters, value £831,266; and bran and pollard, 5,512 tons, valued at £27,888, or together a total of £1,678,549 sterling.

The following table exhibits the remarkable development of this the most important branch of local industry. Giving the quantities exported will prove more useful than a statement merely showing the value, and furnish a more correct basis upon which to estimate the extent of substantial progress made by the agriculturists during the past decade :—

Years.	Flour.		Bran and Pollard.		Wheat.	
	Quantity.	Value.	Quantity.	Value.	Quantity.	Value.
	Tons.	£	Tons.	£	Qrs.	£
1866	30,496	498,024	2,500	18,517	46,756	126,601
1867	43,703	498,222	3,274	14,549	301,543	521,690
1868	23,591	405,982	1,787	10,841	55,876	148,603
1869	38,653	495,589	2,847	15,303	195,031	371,221
1870	27,371	354,012	2,167	12,210	47,079	99,600
1871	46,842	594,482	3,816	14,495	315,054	639,348
1872	38,319	510,826	2,220	9,525	157,678	333,890
1873	57,170	737,160	1,477	7,906	479,702	965,577
1874	58,635	783,489	2,461	15,563	192,308	428,753
1875	76,209	819,395	5,512	27,888	479,882	831,266

The total exports of colonial produce in breadstuffs and grain during the period referred to was—of flour, 440,989 tons, of the value of .£5,698,081; of wheat, 2,270,909 quarters, of the value of £4,466,549; and of bran and pollard, 28,121 tons, of the value of £146,797. Diagram C (page 64) shows the prices of wheat at Port Adelaide in each month during the past ten years.

The quality of South Australian wheat and flour is of such excellence as to command the highest price in the markets of the world. The great bulk of the crop is shipped to the United Kingdom, the daily fluctuations in whose markets are made known here by telegram. New South Wales, Queensland, Cape Town, Mauritius, New Caledonia, and several Eastern ports also receive considerable consignments of South Australian flour.

The harvest of 1875-6—now in course of being garnered— is expected to yield 230,000 tons of breadstuffs beyond local requirements for food and seed; or an excess, available for export, of the value of two and a quarter millions sterling.

WOOL.—That pastoral pursuits are being conducted with great success in South Australia is illustrated by the statement furnished on page 62, showing the export of wool during the last ten years.

It will be remarked that the export of wool has increased fifty per cent. during the past five years, and doubled during the decade. The total value of South Australian wool shipped

C.

SOUTH AUSTRALIA.

DIAGRAM SHOWING WHEAT PRICES AT PORT ADELAIDE FOR TEN YEARS.

Year	Exports		
1866	WHEAT—8,312	FLOUR—30,496	TONS 38,808
1867	WHEAT—53,807	FLOUR—43,703	TONS 97,810
1868	WHEAT—9,933	FLOUR—23,591	TONS 33,524
1869	WHEAT—34,672	FLOUR—38,653	TONS 73,325
1870	WHEAT—8,370	FLOUR—27,370	TONS 35,740
1871	WHEAT—56,670	FLOUR—46,760	TONS 103,430
1872	WHEAT—26,629	FLOUR—34,738	TONS 61,367
1873	WHEAT—58,114	FLOUR—103,543	TONS 161,657
1874	WHEAT—42,363	FLOUR—58,000	TONS 100,363
1875	WHEAT—95,982	FLOUR—76,209	TONS 172,191

in 1856 was £412,163; in 1866, £990,173; and in 1875 it reached £1,833,519 sterling.

Years.	S. A. Wool.	Other Wool.	No. of Bales.	Total Weight.	Total Value.
	Lbs.	Lbs.		Lbs.	£
1866	19,730,523	1,168,562	61,977	20,908,085	1,064,486
1867	19,350,195	3,283,597	66,395	22,633,792	1,144,341
1868	28,899,190	730,335	86,913	29,629,525	1,346,523
1869	27,022,671	3,510,141	87,150	30,522,812	1,128,568
1870	24,169,256	2,049,028	87,394	26,218,284	1,000,344
1871	31,250,677	1,405,750	97,532	32,656,427	1,350,689
1872	33,709,717	940,914	100,017	34,650,631	1,692,609
1873	32,967,941	3,005,493	105,306	35,973,434	1,808,622
1874	35,593,805	4,250,219	114,845	39,844,024	1,998,939
1875	39,723,249	4,785,425	126,046	44,508,674	2,066,227

The aggregate number of bales shipped last year was 126,046, as against 87,394 in 1870, and 61,977 in 1866.

Considering the vast extent of available territory at present unoccupied in South Australia, there would appear to be little doubt that the extraordinary progress already made in the production of wool will steadily continue. The excellent quality of the staple, the great suitability of the climate, giving almost complete immunity from scab, fluke, and other diseases peculiar to sheep, taken together with the security of tenure enjoyed by the pastoral lessees, conduce to the rapid development of this profitable industry.

COPPER.—South Australia owes no little of its prosperity to the employment of a large number of its people, directly and indirectly, in the working of her copper mines, several of which, whilst supporting a very considerable section of the colonists, have been exceedingly profitable to the proprietors. The principal mines are the Burra, the Wallaroo, and the Moonta. From the first of these, 215,000 tons of ore were raised during 31 years from the commencement of operations, producing four millions sterling. The total amount expended by the company was £1,982,000, of which £1,568,000 represented wages, the gross profits being £882,000. Since the opening of the Wallaroo Mines, the total quantity of ore raised therefrom has been 290,000 tons, and the average of the past five years has

E

been 26,000 tons. The Moonta mines were discovered in 1861, since which year 255,000 tons of ore have been raised, realizing £2,760,000. A profit of £928,000 has been divided amongst the shareholders of this magnificent property.

In 1844, shortly after the discovery of copper in South Australia, the total value of the minerals exported was £6436; in 1851 it reached to £310,916; in 1861 it amounted to £454,172; in 1871, to £648,569; and in 1875, to £762,386.

The following table exhibits the steady productiveness of South Australian mines, distinguishes the quantity of fine copper shipped from the quantity of ore exported in its crude state, and gives the estimated value of each.

Years.	Fine Copper.		Copper Ore.		Total Value, all Minerals.
	Cwt.	£	Tons.	£	£
1866	129,272	584,509	16,824	225,683	824,501
1867	156,863	627,384	11,430	113,409	753,413
1868	104,227	400,691	20,725	207,519	624,022
1869	92,788	371,566	26,835	250,259	627,152
1870	109,421	394,919	20,886	173,861	574,090
1871	127,911	518,080	20,127	119,903	648,569
1872	149,050	680,714	26,964	122,020	806,364
1873	141,744	635,131	27,382	133,371	770,590
1874	132,587	557,306	22,854	136,530	700,323
1875	136,835	578,065	26,436	175,101	762,386

The smelting works in connection with these mines are of a very extensive and costly character, employing a large amount of skilled labour.

MISCELLANEOUS PRODUCTS.—In addition to the chief staples above referred to, a variety of minor articles of produce are annually exported, last year amounting in the aggregate to the value of £174,634, including the following principal items. viz. :—Tallow, 25,670 cwt., £38,511 value ; Preserved Meats, 1,259,820 lbs., £28,241 ; Leather, £4410 ; Hides and Skins, £16,139; Wine, 59,174 gallons, £19,240; Bark, 2650 tons, £14,552; Eggs, £7987 ; Dried and Fresh Fruits, £4977 ; Jams and Preserves, £3216 ; Potatoes, 735 tons, £3178; Soap, 1533 cwt., £1804; Salt, 80 tons; Gum, £1251; Slate, £1253 ; and other articles of less value.

SHIPPING.

The rapid growth of the external commerce of South Australia necessitates the employment of a largely increased amount of shipping, as will be seen from the following returns. No less than 844 vessels entered inwards in 1875, of a total capacity of 316,823 tons, and with crews numbering 15,644 men; giving a daily average of 1000 tons register for every working-day throughout the year. Of 95 vessels, having an aggregate carrying capacity of 50,000 tons, lately in Port Adelaide on one day, were the following:—Steamers—one of 1300 tons, three between 400 and 550 tons, and three under 250 tons; ships and barques—one of 2128 tons, one of 1777 tons, six of 1000 to 1500 tons, nineteen between 500 and 1000 tons, and twenty-five between 200 and 500 tons—besides eight brigs, twelve schooners, and sixteen coasters. The subjoined abstracts relate only to vessels arriving at or departing from South Australian ports from or to other countries, and is exclusive of a large number of steam and sailing vessels employed solely in the coasting trade of the Colony.

The following figures represent the aggregate number of vessels inwards and outwards, and the total registered tonnage in the years specified :—

Years.	Number of Vessels.	Tonnage.
1851	538	155,002
1856	867	230,390
1861	788	199,331
1866	1,039	339,871
1871	1,238	373,624
1875	1,634	611,381

It will be noted that the increase in the shipping during the last five years has amounted to no less than seventy per cent. In addition to the chief port of the Colony (Port Adelaide), at which two-thirds of the foreign shipping trade is carried on, there are many outports from which there is a direct export trade with other countries. It has been elsewhere mentioned that the configuration of the coast-line, and the numerous shipping ports, enable vessels of considerable tonnage to be

laden with wheat, wool, and other produce of the adjacent
districts within a short distance of the place of production.
The following table shows the shipping business done at each
of these ports :—

Names of Ports.	Vessels.			Tonnage.			Crew.		
	Inwards.	Outwards.	Total.	Inwards.	Outwards.	Total.	Inwards.	Outwards.	Total.
Port Adelaide ...	489	418	907	205,998	169,706	375,204	7,550	6,446	13,996
Port Augusta ...	1	8	9	92	5,790	5,882	6	151	157
Port Broughton	2	4	6	1,935	2,658	4,593	39	58	97
Port Caroline ...	31	31	62	8,553	8,863	17,416	689	701	1,390
Port Glenelg ...	26	26	52	28,821	29,680	58,501	3,498	3,645	7,143
Port MacDonnell	69	71	140	15,515	15,511	31,062	1,256	1,257	2,513
Port Moonta ...	1	1	2	65	44	109	4	4	8
Murray River...	98	86	184	6,425	5,786	12,211	593	516	1,109
Port Noarlunga	—	2	2	—	373	373	—	17	17
Port Pirie ...	14	23	37	5,776	10,934	16,710	146	280	426
Port Robe ...	26	26	52	8,654	6,854	15,508	612	612	1,224
Port Victor ...	14	10	24	4,802	4,619	9,421	377	214	591
Port Wakefield	7	12	19	3,810	6,221	10,031	100	165	265
Port Wallaroo ...	64	65	129	26,003	26,920	52,923	760	757	1,517
Port Willunga	1	6	7	167	892	1,059	7	39	46
Port Yankalilla	1	1	2	207	207	414	7	7	14
Totals	844	790	1,634	316,823	294,558	611,381	15,644	14,869	30,513

The above return includes the number of steamers arriving
at and departing from ports on the River Murray, the arrivals
numbering eighty-six, and the departures ninety-eight, during
the year.

THE RIVER MURRAY TRADE.

South Australian enterprise opened the River Murray to
navigation in 1853, as well as, at a later period, its great
tributaries, the Darling and the Murrumbidgee. Since the
opening of these rivers the whole of that immense tract of
pastoral country known as Riverina has been heavily stocked,
producing now about two hundred thousand bales of wool
annually. The Murray is navigable for a distance of 2000
miles from its mouth at Goolwa. The Darling, from its junc-
tion at Wentworth, is navigable to Fort Bourke, 800 miles,
and for a short period some 300 miles further into Queensland. The Murrumbidgee, entering the Murray some 300
miles from Wentworth, is navigable to Wagga, a distance of
700 miles, to which town railway communication with Sydney

will shortly be extended. Forty steamers and fifty barges are occupied in the trade. At present, the larger portion of the upper river traffic is diverted up-stream to Echuca, and thence by railway to Melbourne, owing to special inducements held out by the Victorian Government, who convey wool over that line at less than cost. As, however, the natural advantages of down-stream navigation are so great, saving £2 or £3 per ton in freight, as compared with the railway route, there is little doubt that the bulk of the carrying trade will eventually revert to South Australia. Surveys are being made, and proceedings taken for opening the Murray Mouth to large vessels, alongside which the river boats will then discharge.

RAILWAYS.

Including those just approaching completion, there are three hundred and seventy-one miles of railway in South Australia, three hundred miles of which are worked by loco-motives. The following table shows the length of the several lines and their termini :—

	Locomotive.	Horse traction.
GOVERNMENT LINES—		
Adelaide and Port Adelaide, including wharf lines	9½	—
Adelaide, Gawler, Kapunda. and Burra	124	—
Strathalbyn, Goolwa. and Port Victor	—	32
Port Wakefield and Blyth's Plains	42	—
Port Wakefield and Wallaroo	34½	—
Port Pirie and Gladstone	32	—
Port Broughton	—	14
Lacepede Bay and Naracoorte	51	—
Total ...	293	46
PRIVATE COMPANIES' LINES—		
Adelaide and Glenelg	7	—
Kadina, Wallaroo, and Moonta	—	25
Grand Total	300	71

The cost of construction of the lines at present in working has been £1,155,267. They are single lines, of five-foot three-inch gauge. Sixty miles are laid with rails sixty-five pounds to the yard, and the remainder with rails of forty pounds to the yard. In addition, the cost of rolling stock and other plant amounted to £221,918, making a total of £1,337,185. The cost of construction, exclusive of rolling stock, was, for the Adelaide and Port Railway, £17,433 per mile; for the Kapunda Railway, £11,191; and for the extension to the Burra, £5072. The rolling stock on the Government lines consists of the following :—Twenty-nine locomotives, fifty-one passenger carriages, and six hundred and thirty-three goods waggons of all descriptions.

The estimated cost of the one hundred and forty-six miles approaching completion is £667,000—the average cost being £4600 per mile.

Up to the close of 1874, the total receipts amounted to £1,772,376; the working expenses to £1,066,937, reconstruction to £104,147, and maintenance to £420,500, leaving a balance of £180,789 to profit.

The receipts for the year 1874 amounted to £132,806, and the expenditure to £124,610, showing a balance of £8196 towards meeting interest on cost of construction.

The following statement shows the amount of goods and passenger traffic, and the total receipts at intervals of five years :—

Years.	Miles open.	Passenger Traffic.	Goods Traffic.	Total Receipts.
		No.	Tons.	£
1856	7½	241,886	26,354	19,498
1861	58	306,140	138,663	90,489
1866	58	405,502	161,671	114,131
1871	133	384,389	211,683	110,963
1875	133	386,117	301,530	166,710

The mileage run by trains in 1866 was 128,957; in 1871, 275,131; and it increased to 386,117 in 1875.

The two lines worked by horse traction are, together, forty-six miles in length; the train mileage run was 135,316, the total receipts £9387, and the working expenses £9037 : the number of passengers carried was 31,895, and of goods 30,370 tons. The rolling stock consists of fourteen passenger carriages, and 185 goods trucks, and fifty-six horses are employed.

The average charge for carrying passengers on the Government railways ranges from 1d. to 1½d. per mile, and the charge for carrying a ton of goods one mile is 2¼d. to 2¾d. A bushel of wheat is carried from the Burra to Port Adelaide, a distance of one hundred miles, for 7d.—before the construction of the railway it cost double. A ton of ore is now brought from the Burra Mines to Port Adelaide for 21s., whereas, prior to the opening of the line, it cost 35s. to 40s. to convey it to a port of shipment.

The policy pursued has been to reduce the cost of carriage to a minimum, with a view of developing the resources of the agricultural and mining districts through which the lines of railway pass. Without railway communication the limit within which wheat could be profitably grown would have been reached many years ago, and the quantities now produced could not be brought to a place of shipment except by steam power. As much as twelve hundred tons of wheat has sometimes to be brought down in a day. Although the railways only yield a return but little in excess of the cost of working, and maintaining them in good order, the facilities and cheapness of transit more than counterbalance the burthen of interest which falls upon the general public, who benefit in a direct ratio by the prosperity of the producing interests. Frequent communication between distant places situated on the lines of railway is secured to an extent which a private company having to realize dividends could not possibly afford.

Two railways have been constructed by private companies —one is a line connecting Adelaide with Glenelg, a populous watering-place, at which the ocean mail steamers call on their arrival from and departure for Suez. This line, under seven miles in length (single line, 5-foot 3-inch gauge), cost in construction £15,875, or about £2200 a mile. The great passenger traffic and frequency of communication necessitate the use of a large proportion of rolling stock as compared with the length of the line. It consists of four locomotives and eighteen passenger carriages. The total cost, including rolling stock, amounted to £33,432. The traffic receipts since the line was opened in August 1873 have amounted to

£25,911, and the working expenses, including maintenance, to £13,870, showing a balance of £12,041 to profit of the undertaking. The working expenses amounted to fifty-three per cent. of the receipts.

The other private line connects the Wallaroo and Moonta Mines with the sea-board at Port Wallaroo. It is twenty-five miles long, and is worked by horse traction. The original capital was £60,000, on which twenty per cent. has been divided during each of the past ten years. The present value of the property is £90,000, the difference having accrued from profits expended in improving and extending the works, which include jetty accommodation.

ROADS.

Large sums of money have been expended on the construction and maintenance of main trunk lines of road in the settled districts, through which there are 2700 miles defined. During the past twenty years, about £1,750,000 have been devoted to these works, and, with the exception of £200,000, the whole cost has been defrayed from the general revenue, no special toll or rate having been levied. The aggregate number of miles macadamised is 884, which are maintained in good order. In addition to the main lines, perhaps as many more miles of district or by-roads have been constructed and kept in repair by local municipalities. For this purpose funds are raised by a rate on landed property, supplemented by grants-in-aid from the general revenue. Fifty miles of metalled streets have already been formed in the City of Adelaide alone. The average cost of construction and metalling main roads is estimated to be £1000 per mile, and of maintaining them in repair £60 to £100 per mile annually.

WATERWORKS.

Considerable attention has been paid to the subject of water supply, which was first undertaken as a public work in 1857. In addition to a high-pressure supply to the city and suburbs of Adelaide, water has been laid on to several other centres of population, among which are Port Adelaide, Glenelg, Port

Augusta, Port Pirie, Port Elliot, Kadina, and Moonta. The River Torrens is the source of supply to the city and suburban townships Port Adelaide and Glenelg. The water is collected in a masonry dam, from which it passes by means of an aqueduct three and a quarter miles in length, into two reservoirs, the larger of which has a water area of 167 acres, with a storage capacity of 945 millions of gallons. The smaller reservoir has a water area of twenty-seven and a half acres, and contains 140 millions of gallons. The supply is conveyed to the city by an eighteen-inch main, five miles in length. The primary mains are from fifteen to twenty-one inches in diameter, of a total length of nine miles; the secondary mains are from ten to fifteen inches, and fourteen miles long; and the street mains are from three to ten inches, of a length of 134 miles. The furthest point of supply is sixteen miles distant from the reservoirs. From these sources over fifty thousand people are supplied. The highest water level of the reservoir is one hundred and seventy feet above the highest point in the city, and three hundred feet above the sea. Ample provision is made for the suppression of fire, hydrants being laid throughout every street and road, at intervals of about four chains apart.

The total amount of the loans raised for the construction of waterworks is £620,000. The receipts amounted to £14,651 in 1865; to £22,600 in 1871; and to £30,895 in 1875. The charges for water have been reduced from time to time, the rate for that supplied through meters being now eighteenpence per thousand gallons.

POSTAL COMMUNICATION.

Great attention has been devoted to the subject of postal communication. Considering the thinly peopled and extensive area of the outlying settled districts, more than ordinary facilities are afforded the public by frequent and rapid despatch of inland mails. A uniform rate of twopence per half-ounce is charged upon letters carried to places within the Province, and a like rate for letters posted to the sister Colonies of Austral-

asia, whether by overland mail thrice a week, or by the regular
intercolonial steam communication by sea. No charge is made
for the carriage of newspapers, either inland or to any part of
the world, so far as the South Australian Post Office is con-
cerned. Book packets and parcels are carried at a low rate,
and the system is extensively used. The direct four-weekly
mail communication with Europe and the East, under contract
with the Peninsular and Oriental Steam Navigation Company,
is performed on an average under forty days from London to
Adelaide with great punctuality. The following table shows
the rapid extension of postal communication, a sure criterion
of progress :—

Years.	No. of Post Offices.	Miles travelled by Mails.	No. of		Income.
			Letters.	Newspapers.	
1856	102	—	844,853	785,608	£ 8,925
1866	226	809,160	2,703,105	1,968,120	27,987
1875	357	1,542,426	4,431,525	2,950,997	43,205

Taking the last ten years, it will be remarked that the
number of Post Offices has increased from 226 to 357; of
distance travelled by the mails, from 809,160 to 1,542,426
miles; of letters, from 2,703,105 to 4,431,525; and of newspapers, from 1,968,120 to 2,950,997. The income of the
Department has been as follows :—In the year 1856, £8925;
in 1866, £27,987; and in 1875, £43,205.

The Money Order system is in full operation in all the
principal towns of the Colony, there being eighty-two offices
in all. Money Orders are also issued and paid in connection
with Great Britain and Ireland, Germany, Canada, and all the
Australian Colonies. The system of Telegraphic Money
Orders is also availed of to a large extent. The orders issued
in 1874 numbered 18,879, of £61,190 value; and 13,072 were
paid, amounting to £42,282.

TELEGRAPHS.

The geographical position of South Australia being practically that of the most western of the group, the first port of arrival and the last of departure for mail communication with Great Britain and the East, necessitated early and earnest attention being devoted to the extension of the South Australian telegraphs, so as to afford instantaneous communication with Melbourne, Sydney, and Brisbane. After this work had been accomplished by the several Governments, the question of direct telegraphic communication with Europe naturally became one of great moment to South Australia, she having under her control that portion of the continent from south to north through which an overland line could best be carried. In order to accomplish this vast undertaking, from which such great results have flowed, and an immense area of territory opened up for settlement, South Australia, at her own risk and cost—which has amounted to over £370,000—determined to enter upon the work of erecting a line of telegraph some 2200 miles in length, across a continent which had only been traversed by an exploring party.

The first local line of thirty-six miles of telegraph was laid twenty years ago, and the receipts of the department were £366. In 1858 intercolonial communication was opened by the addition of 350 miles. In 1861 the total length of wire open was 914 miles, and the receipts were £7382. In 1872 the overland line to Port Darwin was completed, when cable communication was established with London. The completion of this work brought the length of wire up to 3731 miles, and the total receipts to £14,684. Every township and port of any importance is connected with the city by means of telegraph, the number of stations open being 105, between which telegrams are sent at a uniform rate of one shilling for ten words, which sum covers the transmission of a message over a distance of a thousand miles. There is a uniform charge of 10s. 6d. a word on messages sent between Adelaide and London. The traffic in 1875 over the transcontinental line in connection with the European cable amounted to £104,205,

the number of messages being 9709. To show the ramifica-
tions of the telegraph system in Australia, it is only needful
to mention that the length of lines open or closely approaching
completion is 28,285 miles; and the number of stations 547.

Colonies.	No. of Stations.	Miles of Wire.
South Australia ...	105	5,004
New South Wales ...	137	7,904
Victoria	163	4,613
Queensland	90	3,617
Tasmania	32	547
Western Australia ...	20	1,600

At the close of the year 1875 there were 3904 miles of
wire open throughout the Colony, and there are 1100 miles
now in course of construction. The 105 stations already
erected employ 230 officers, operators, and messengers. The
number of messages inland and intercolonial transmitted in
the year was 315,342, and international 9709, making a total
of 325,051. The revenue of the year was £33,616, of which
amount £17,083 was derived from inland messages, £4762
from intercolonial and £11,771 from international messages.
The following table shows the operations of the South Australian Telegraph Department from the commencement :—

Years.	No. of Stations.	Miles of Wire Open.	No. of Messages.	Receipts.
				£
1856	7	36	14,738	366
1861	27	914	76,709	7,382
1865	45	1,173	112,344	11,735
1872	86	3,731	170,902	14,684
1875	105	3,904	325,051	33,616

* There is a through communication with all the sister Colonies, Victoria, New South Wales, Tasmania, and Queensland.
The connection of Western Australia with the telegraphic
circle is rapidly being accomplished, when the continent of
Australia will be traversed by wire from north to south and

from east to west. A cable is now being laid to connect New Zealand, thereby completing the chain which will unite the whole of the British possessions at the Antipodes with the Mother Country and the rest of the civilized world.

Daily weather and shipping reports are interchanged between the several ports and principal towns throughout the whole continent.

RATES OF WAGES.

The following compilation, by Mr. J. Kemp Penny, Labour Agent, is taken from the *South Australian Register* newspaper of 29th January 1876. It shows the rates of wages paid in Adelaide to skilled labourers and other tradesmen, the prices varying of course according to the proficiency or skill of the individual and the season of the year. Great care has been taken in every instance to procure authentic information :—

BOOKBINDERS.—30s. to £3 per week ; forwarders, 35s. to 45s. ; finishers, 60s. to 70s.

BOOTMAKERS.—At the principal factories piecework is the rule, but some men are employed on daywork, whose average earnings are 40s. to 45s. per week, while very expert hands earn over £3. Female machine hands receive weekly from 15s. to £1, while girls as tackers, &c. receive from half-a-crown to 15s. The present prices at piecework are as follows:— Men's Goods—Riveting wellingtons and riding boots, 2s. ; half-wellingtons, 1s. 9d. ; side-springs, 1s. 6d. ; strong lace-up, 2s. ; finishing wellingtons and riding boots, 2s. ; half-wellingtons, 1s. 9d. ; side-springs, 1s. 6d. ; strong lace-up, 9d. Women's Goods—Riveting side-springs, plain, 1s. 2d. ; plain leather boots, 1s. ; slippers, 4d. ; finishing side-springs, plain, 1s. 2d. ; plain leather boots, 8d. ; slippers, 3d. Girls (from 10 to 13), calf, riveting side-springs, plain, 9d. ; finishing do., 8d. ; good female fitters from 12s. to 14s.

BRASS-FOUNDERS.—9s. to 12s. per day.

BREWERS.—30s. to 50s. per week.

BRICKMAKERS.—13s. per 1000 on the back.

BUILDERS.—In this trade firms have adopted the eight

hours' system. The prices ruling are—For stonemasons and wallers, 9s. to 10s. per day; stonecutters, 9s. to 9s. 6d.; plasterers, do.; bricklayers, do.; slaters, a shade higher; carpenters, 8s. to 9s.; labourers. 6s. to 7s.; pick and shovel men, do.

BAKERS.—Foremen are receiving from £1 15s. to £2 15s. per week, and second hands from 25s. to £2, with board and lodging; skilled confectioners proportionately higher.

BUTCHERS.—Engagements are made by the week. The present rates are—For shopmen, 35s. to 50s.; youths, 15s. to £1; slaughtermen, 30s. to £2; and small goods men, from 30s. to £2 5s., with board.

BASKETMAKERS.—Piecework make wages from 50s. to £3 7s. per week, mostly canework.

CABINETMAKERS.—Engagements are chiefly made by piecework, but when by time the following are the customary rates per day of eight and a half hours:—First-class workmen, 9s. to 10s.; second do., 8s.; upholsterers, 8s. 6d. to 10s.; makers of deal tables, meat-safes, &c., from 7s. 6d. to 9s.

CARTERS.—25s. to 35s. per week.

COACHBUILDERS.—The wages per week vary according to the following scale :—Smiths, from £3 to £3 10s.; bodymakers, from £2 14s. to £3; wheelers, £2 10s. to £3; painters, £2 to £2 14s.; trimmers, do.; vicemen, £1 10s. to £2.

COOPERS.—Work is chiefly done by the piece; when otherwise, however, the day is understood to consist of eight hours, for which the remuneration varies from 8s. to 9s. In piecework 2s. is paid for a cask of three gallons, 2s. 6d. for five gallons, and 3s. 3d. for one of ten gallons.

COPPERSMITHS.—9s. to 12s. per day.

DRAPERS.—30s. to 70s. per week.

FARRIERS.—Firemen per day of ten hours, 10s.; floormen, from £2 5s. to £2 10s. per week.

GARDENING.—Gardeners, 6s. to 7s. per day; digging, 3d. (sandy soil) to 1s. per rod (ordinary garden soil); trenching, by contract; pruning, 2s. 6d. to 4s. per 100 vines, 6s. to 7s. daywork.

GASFITTERS.—In regular employment the wages vary from

£2 to £3 per week; when employed by the day, they receive from 8s. to 10s.

GALVANIZED TIN IRON WORKERS.—Daywork from 8s. to 10s.; week of 48 hours, £2 2s. to £2 14s.

GUNSMITHS.—9s. to 12s. per day.

IRON-WORKERS.—Boilermakers per day of eight hours get from 10s. to 11s.; smiths, do.; fitters and turners, do.; moulders, do.; labourers, from 6s. 6d. to 7s. 6d.

IRON TRADE.—General smiths, 9s. to 10s. per day; first-class smiths, 9s. per day; fitters, 9s. to 11s. per day; wheel-wrights, 8s. to 11s. per day; moulders (first-class), 9s. per day; painters, 5s. per day; engine-drivers, 7s. to 10s. per day; sawyers, 7s. to 8s. per day; carpenters, 7s. to 11s. per day; turners, 7s. to 8s. per day; foundry hands, 6s. to 7s. per day; labourers, 6s. to 7s. per day.

JEWELLERS.—Ordinary workmen, £2 10s. to £4 10s. per week, and more skilled workmen, engravers, &c., £5 to £6.

MILLERS.—50s. to 60s.

PLUMBERS.—Very good hands obtain from 11s. to 12s. per day of eight hours; inferior workmen, £2 8s. per week.

PAINTERS AND GLAZIERS.—These tradesmen generally receive 8s. to 10s. per day of eight hours, or 1s. to 1s. 3d. per hour. Grainers and writers, 10s. per day, or 1s. 3d. per hour; very good writers and grainers, 11s. to 13s. per day.

PAPERHANGERS.—9d. to 1s. 6d. for 12 yards.

PRINTERS.—Compositors, newspaper, 1s. per 1000; jobbing hands, £2 15s. per week; pressmen £2 15s.

SADDLERS.—Most of the work done in this trade is by the piece, but when by time, the following are the rates:—First-class harness men from 8s. to 9s. per day of 10 hours summer, 9 hours winter; second class or jobbing, from 5s. to 7s. 6d.; first-class saddle hands, from 10s. to 12s.

SAILMAKERS.—1s. 2d. to 1s. 3d. per hour, eight hours per diem.

SEAMEN'S WAGES (Intercolonial) are steady at £5 per month.

STONEBREAKERS.—3s. per yard.

STOREMEN.—30s. to 50s. per week.

TINSMITHS.—11*d*. to 1*s*. 4*d*. per hour.

TAILORS.—Wages, 10*d*. per hour piecework, or 1*s*. per hour daywork. Good workmen are now earning from £4 to £5 per week. Females receive a corresponding increase.

TANNERS AND CURRIERS.—The working day is ten hours. Beamsmen in the lime yard get from £2 to £2 10*s*. per week; strikers and finishers from 36*s*. to 40*s*.; tanners from 36*s*. to 42*s*.; curriers' work is all done by the piece and on agreed conditions. First-rate workmen who have served their full apprenticeship term are earning from £3 10*s*. to £4 10*s*. per week.

WATCHMAKERS.—The wages given vary from £3 10*s*. to £4 per week.

WHEELWRIGHTS.—1*s*. to 1*s*. 3*d*. per hour.

FEMALE DOMESTICS.—Per week, with board and lodging— General servants, 8*s*. to 12*s*.; cooks, 10*s*. to 20*s*.; housemaids, 8*s*. to 12*s*.; kitchenmaids, 8*s*. to 10*s*.; housekeepers, 10*s*. to £1; laundresses, 10*s*. to 16*s*.; nursemaids, 8*s*. to 12*s*.; nursegirls, 4*s*. to 7*s*.; charwomen, 3*s*. to 4*s*. per diem.

SHEARERS.—Shearers, 20*s*. per 100; rollers, 15*s*.; pressers, 25*s*.; sewers, 20*s*.; dumpers, 20*s*.; pickers, 12*s*.; cooks, 40*s*.; butchers, 25*s*.; cooks' mates, 20*s*. per week.

STATION HANDS.—Drovers, £1 to £1 10*s*. per week, or 10*s*. 6*d*. per day and find themselves; boundary-riders, 17*s*. to 25*s*. per week; shepherds, 17*s*. to 20*s*. per week; married couples, per annum, £52 to £75; lambminders, 10*s*. to 15*s*. per week; bullock-drivers, 20*s*. to 25*s*. per week; knockabout hands, 17*s*. to 20*s*. per week; bush carpenters and blacksmiths, 30*s*. per week; cooks, 17*s*. to 25*s*. per week; water-drawers, 18*s*. to 20*s*. per week. All the above are with rations and expenses paid up to the station.

FARM HANDS.—Ploughmen, 20*s*. per week; general farm servants, 20*s*. to 30*s*. per week; married couples, females to cook, &c., 20*s*. to 30*s*. per week; harvesters, 25*s*. to 35*s*. per week; boys, from 10*s*. to 12*s*.; youngsters tailing cattle and sheep, 4*s*. to 8*s*. per week; teamsters, 20*s*. to 30*s*.; hay harvesters, 25*s*. to 35*s*.; all with board and lodging.

MISCELLANEOUS.—Fencers, post and 3-wire fence, £10 to

£20 per mile ; do., per rod, three-rail, 2s. to 3s.; wire do.,
4s. to 7s.; cabmen, 20s. to 30s. per week with board and
lodging; busmen, 35s. to 40s. per week without board;
labourers, 6s. to 8s. per diem without board and lodging;
ostlers, 20s. to 25s. per week with board and lodging. Sawyers,
logs at pit, 13s. per 100.

AVERAGE WAGES OF MINERS.—Moonta District—Miners,
per week, eight hours' shift, £2 2s.; breaksmen do., none
employed; engineers, from £1 16s. to £2 15s.; tribute, £1 18s.
to £2 5s.; on contract, from £1 16s. to £2; owners' account,
5s. 6d. per day.

SCALE OF RATIONS PER WEEK—10 lbs. flour, 12 lbs. meat,
2 lbs. sugar, ¼ lb. tea.

PRICES OF PROVISIONS.

The following are the current quotations in Adelaide, as
taken from the public prints, of live stock, farm and garden
produce, provisions, groceries, &c. :—

WHOLESALE, FLOUR, GRAIN, &c.

	£	s.	d.	£	s.	d.
Flour, fine silk-dressed, per ton of 2000 lbs., at the Port, bags included	11	0	0 to	11	5	0
Ditto ditto, country brand	10	5	0 ,,	11	0	0
Wheat, per bushel of 60 lbs., large lots, at the Port (old)	0	5	0	—		
Ditto ditto (new)	0	4	8 ,,	0	4	9
Bran, per bushel of 20 lbs., at the Port, bags included	0	1	2 ,,	0	1	2½
Pollard, per bushel of 20 lbs.	0	0	11 ,.	0	1	0
Oats, per bushel of 40 lbs., without bags	0	4	0 .,	0	4	6
Barley, per bushel of 50 lbs., without bags	0	5	6 ,,	0	6	0

WHOLESALE, DAIRY AND FARM PRODUCE.

		£	s.	d.	
Bacon	per lb.	0	0	10	—
Butter	per lb.	0	0	10	—
Ditto (Potted)	per lb.	0	0	11	—
Cheese	per lb.	0	0	9	—
Eggs	per doz.	0	0	9½	—
Hams	per lb.	0	0	11	—
Lard	per lb.	0	0	9	—
Onions	per. cwt.	0	11	0	—
Honey	per lb.	0	0	3	—
Hay	per ton	3	10	0	—
Prairie grass	per bush.	0	8	0	—
Seed, Lucerne	per lb.	0	1	2	—
Peas	per bush.	0	3	6	—
Vetches	per bush.	0	8	0	—

F

HIDES, SKINS, BONES, &c.

			£	s.	d.		£	s.	d.
Hides, salted ...	... ...	per lb.	0	0	4½	to	0	0	5
Butchers' Green	... ...	each	1	5	0	,,	2	10	0
Hoofs	... ...	per ton	1	10	0	,,	2	10	0
Green Kangaroo Skins	... ...	per doz.	0	7	0	,,	2	5	0
Skins, Calf	... ...	each	0	1	4	.,	0	10	0
Ditto, Wallaby	... ...	per doz.	0	10	0	,,	1	15	0
Shank Bones	... ...	per ton	5	0	0	,,	10	0	0

BARK.

			£	s.	d.		£	s.	d.
Bark, Wattle, ground	... ...	per ton	7	0	0		—		
Ditto, ditto, chopped	... ...	per ton	5	10	0	to	6	0	0

TALLOW.

			£	s.	d.				
Tallow, Beef, for Export	... ...	per ton	32	0	0		—		
Ditto, Mutton, ditto	... ...	per ton	34	0	0		—		

WOOL.

			£	s.	d.		£	s.	d.
Washed	... ...	per lb.	0	0	11	to	0	1	2
Greasy...	... ...	per lb.	0	0	7	,,	0	0	8

WINE (COLONIAL).

			£	s.	d.		£	s.	d.
Good sound Colonial Wine of last year's vintage, for large quantities in bulk	... ...	per gall.	0	1	6	to	0	4	0
Superior ditto	... ...	per gall.	0	5	0	,,	0	10	0
Colonial Spirits, in bond	... ...	per gall.	0	3	6		—		

LEATHER.

			£	s.	d.		£	s.	d.
Basils	... ...	per doz.	0	15	0	to	1	0	0
Colonial Calf...	... ...	per lb.	0	4	0	,,	0	5	6
Ditto Kip	... ...	per lb.	0	2	3	,,	0	2	6
Ditto Sole ...	... ...	per lb.	0	1	2	.,	0	1	7
Ditto Kangaroo	... ...	per doz.	1	15	0	.,	4	0	0
Ditto Wallaby	... ...	per lb.	0	12	0	,,	0	14	0

COPPER.

			£	s.	d.				
Wallaroo	... ...	per ton	82	0	0		—		
Burra ...	... ...	per ton	82	0	0		—		

LIVE STOCK.

			£	s.	d.		£	s.	d.
Horses, Draught	... ...		30	0	0	to	45	0	0
Ditto, Light ...	... ...		12	0	0	.,	20	0	0
Bullocks, Fat...	... ...		10	0	0	,,	15	0	0

Sheep, Fat Wethers, 12s. to 17s., according to season.

RETAIL FARM AND DAIRY PRODUCE.

Quotations:— Bread and Flour—Bread, 2½d. to 3½d. per 2-lb. loaf; do., aërated, 3d. 2-lb. loaf; flour, 1½d. to 2d. per lb. Butcher's meat—Beef, 4d. to 8d. per lb.; mutton, 2d. to 5d.; lamb, 2s. 6d. to 3s. 6d. per quarter; pork, 7d. to 8d.; veal, 5d. to 8d. Dairy produce—Bacon, 1s. to 1s. 2d. per lb.; butter, fresh, 1s. 2d.; do., salted, 1s. 2d.; cheese, 1s.; eggs, 1s. per dozen; fowls, 5s. per pair; ducks, 6s. to 6s. 6d. per pair; geese, 6s. each; hams, 1s. 2d. per lb.; honey, 5d. per lb.; lard, 1s. per lb.; milk, 4d. to 6d. per quart; pigeons, 1s. 3d. to 1s. 5d. per pair; rabbits, tame, 1s. each; wild do., 1s. per pair; turkeys, 6s. to 10s. each.

GROCERIES.

Tea, 2s. to 2s. 6d. per lb.; sugar, 3d. to 4½d. per lb.; coffee, 1s. 6d. per lb.; rice, 3d. to 5d. per lb.; salt, 1d. per lb.; tobacco, 4s. to 4s. 6d.; soap, 3d. to 4d. per lb.

HAY MARKET.

Best wheaten hay, £1 10s. per ton; good mixed do., £3 15s.

EAST-END MARKET.

Vegetables — Beans (broad), 2s. to 2s. 6d. per bushel; beans (French), 1s. 3d. to 2s. per dozen lbs.; beetroot, 1s. to 1s. 6d. per dozen; cabbages, 1s. 6d. to 4s. per dozen; do. (Savoys), 2s. to 3s. per dozen; capsicums, 1s. to 1s. 3d. per lb.; carrots, 1s. 6d. to 2s. per dozen bunches; cauliflowers, 3s. to 5s. per dozen; celery, 4s. to 6s. per dozen heads; chillies, 1s. to 1s. 3d. per lb.; horse-radish, 6d. to 10d. per lb.; garlic, 4d. to 6d. per lb.; lettuces, 6d. to 1s. 3d. per dozen; marjoram, 6d. to 8d. per dozen bunches; mint, 6d. per dozen bunches; onions, 6s. 6d. to 8s. 6d. per cwt.; parsnips, 1s. 6d. to 2s. 6d. per dozen bunches; peas, 3s. to 4s. per bushel; potatoes, 4s. 6d. to 5s. per cwt.; radishes, 6d. to 8d. per dozen bunches; do. (turnip), 6d. to 8d. per dozen bunches; rhubarb, 2s. to 3s. per dozen lbs.; sage, 6d. to 8d. per dozen bunches; shalots, 4d. to 6d. per lb.; thyme, 6d. to 8d. per dozen bunches; tomatoes, 1s. 6d. to 2s. per dozen lbs.; trombones, 4s. to 7s. per dozen; turnips, 1s. 6d. to 2s. per dozen bunches; vegetable marrows, 1s. 6d. to 3s. per dozen; watercress, 6d. to 8d. per dozen bunches; cucumbers, 6d. to 3s. per dozen. Fruit — Almonds (green), 2d. per lb.; do. (hard-shell), 2d. per lb.; do. (soft-shell), 6d. per lb.; do. (cracked), 8d. per lb.; apples, 1s. 6d. to 3s. 6d. per bushel; apricots, 20s. to 22s. per cwt.; do., 2d. to 6d. per dozen; Barcelona nuts, 7s. per dozen lbs.; citrons, 15s. per cwt.; damsons, 2s. 6d. to 3s. per bushel; figs, 2d. to 6d. per dozen; gooseberries (Cape), 9d. to 10d. per lb.; grapes, 1s. 6d. to 2s. per dozen lbs.; lemons, 9d. to 2s. per dozen; melons (water), 15s. to 18s. per cwt.; nectarines, 2d. to 3d. per dozen; oranges, 1s. to 2s. 6d. per dozen; peaches, 2d. to 6d. per dozen; pears, 2s. 6d. to 4s. per bushel; plums, 3s. to 4s. per bushel; strawberries, 6d. to 8d. per lb. Dairy produce — Bacon, 10d. per lb.; do. (green), 9d. per lb.; butter (fresh), 10d. to 1s. per lb.; cheese (English), 1s. 6d. to 1s. 8d. per lb.; do. (colonial), 7d. to 8d. per lb.; dairy pork. 8d. per lb.; ducks, 4s. to 4s. 6d. per pair; eggs, 11d. to 1s. per dozen; fowls, 3s. 6d. to 4s. per pair; geese, 4s. to 4s. 6d. each; ham, 1s. to 1s. 1d. per lb.; lard, 9d. per lb.; turkeys, 5s. to 9s. each. Miscellaneous — Beeswax, 10d. to 1s. 2d. per lb.; colonial wine, 2s. to 6s. per gallon; colonial jam, 5d. to 7d. per lb.; flowers, 2d. to 1s. per bunch; honey, 32s. to 34s. per cwt.; rabbits, 1s. to 1s. 6d. per pair; pigeons, 1s. 3d. to 1s. 6d. per pair.

The rent of a dwelling suitable for an artisan and his family in Adelaide or the immediate suburbs varies from six to fifteen shillings per week, but in the country towns the rate is less. Large numbers of artisans, however, reside in their own freehold cottages. The savings of a few years have in many instances sufficed to enable them to accomplish this. Land is cheap, and the necessary advances for the erection of dwellings are readily obtainable from the several Building Societies. Cottages, with fuel and water, are provided for ploughmen, shepherds, and other labourers employed on farms or sheep-runs. The following are quoted rates for house rent and for board and lodging :—

House Rent.

Two rooms, 4s. to 6s.; three rooms, 6s. to 10s.; four rooms, 8s. to 15s.; six rooms, 12s. to 25s. free from taxes; single room, 2s. 6d.; ditto (furnished) 6s. to 9s. per week. Gas is 8s. to 12s. per 1000 cubic feet, and water laid on 1s. 6d. per 1000 gallons.

Board and Lodging.

Per week at Bushmen's Club, 18s.; at private houses, for single young men, shopmen, &c., 15s. to 18s.; clerks, &c., 20s. to 30s.; single females, 10s. to 15s.; private lodgers at hotels, 20s. to 4l. 4s.

Wearing apparel is procurable at the under-mentioned prices :—

Working men's black cloth suits, 39s. to 90s.; every day wear, 29s. to 65s.; moleskin trousers, 6s. 6d. to 10s. 6d.; tweed suit, 29s. to 80s.; jacket, 13s. to 40s.; waistcoat, 5s. to 11s.; trousers, 8s. to 25s.; boys' clothes, 15s. to 40s. per suit.

METEOROLOGICAL.

The following tables give the mean monthly rainfall at Adelaide during the thirty-six years 1839–74, and the result of the Meteorological Observations made at the Observatory during the ten years 1865–74 :—

Months.	Rainfall (36 Years, 1839–74).				Mean Evaporation, Five Years.
	Mean.	Mean No. of Wet Days.	Greatest.	Least.	
	Inches.				Inches.
January	0·722	4	4·000	0·000	10·641
February	0·670	3	3·100	0·000	8·802
March	0·881	5½	3·753	0·000	7·608
April	1·760	8½	6·780	0·250	4·474
May	2·814	13	6·340	0·690	2·902
June	2·915	14	7·800	1·138	1·795
July	2·801	16	5·380	0·726	1·959
August	2·621	16	6·240	0·675	2·667
September ...	2·071	13½	4·610	0·711	3·427
October	1·739	10	3·834	0·460	5·981
November ...	1·263	5	3·550	0·100	6·979
December ...	0·894	5½	3·977	0·105	9·420
	21·091	114	—	—	66·655

For the Ten Years 1865-1874.

Months.	Barometer corrected and reduced to 32°. Mean, 9 A.M.	Highest.	Lowest.	Temperature. Dry Bulb. Mean.	Maximum.	Minimum.	Mean Highest during the Day.	Mean Lowest during Night.	Mean Diurnal Range.	Wet Bulb. Average No. of Days' Temp. exceeded 90°.	Mean Temperature of Evaporation.	Solar Radiation. Mean Highest in Sun.	Actual Highest in Sun.	Terrestrial Radiation. Mean Lowest on Wool.	Actual Lowest on Wool.
January ...	29·813	30·152	29·245	73·7	113·5	47·1	86·4	61·0	25·4	10	61·6	135·2	164·0	53·9	38·5
February ...	29·860	30·250	29·347	73·8	110·0	47·5	86·3	61·4	24·9	10	61·8	134·1	158·3	53·6	37·5
March ...	29·979	30·301	29·430	70·1	107·8	46·5	81·8	58·5	23·3	7	59·4	130·1	155·2	51·5	36·5
April ...	30·010	30·365	29·404	64·6	98·0	41·9	74·5	54·8	19·7	1	56·7	120·7	146·3	47·3	32·5
May ...	30·002	30·517	29·366	58·2	88·3	38·0	66·2	50·1	16·1	0	52·8	109·8	134·0	43·2	28·0
June ...	29·998	30·533	29·191	54·4	76·0	37·0	61·4	47·4	14·0	0	50·3	101·1	125·7	41·0	25·0
July... ...	30·020	30·503	29·168	51·5	72·5	31·2	58·8	44·1	14·7	0	47·8	103·6	121·4	38·0	24·1
August ...	29·945	30·492	29·110	53·7	80·0	34·1	62·3	45·2	17·1	0	49·3	111·1	130·5	38·2	26·4
September .	29·920	30·383	29·096	56·9	84·7	35·3	66·4	47·3	19·1	0	51·2	117·0	138·4	40·3	25·1
October ...	29·942	30·350	29·207	62·5	100·0	38·1	74·0	51·1	22·9	2	51·3	124·1	151·1	44·0	24·0
November..	29·880	30·364	29·223	66·5	113·5	40·9	78·7	51·3	24·4	4	57·0	121·9	160·5	47·2	29·2
December..	29·809	30·167	29·185	71·4	112·0	46·5	83·8	58·7	25·1	9	59·3	133·2	150·0	50·9	35·0
Year ...	29·936	30·533	29·096	63·1	113·5	31·2	73·4	52·8	20·6	43	55·1	120·8	164·0	45·8	24·6

From which the following hygrometric results are deduced : —

	Temperature of Dew Point. Degrees.	Elastic Force of Vapour. Inches.	Degree of Humidity. (Saturation = 100.)
January	52·8	0·400	48
February	53·0	0·405	48
March	51·1	0·377	51
April	50·2	0·363	60
May	47·9	0·335	67
June	46·3	0·313	74
July	44·0	0·289	77
August	45·0	0·298	73
September	46·0	0·310	66
October	47·3	0·326	57
November	49·3	0·352	54
December	50·1	0·362	47
Year	48·3	0·338 -	60

CONCLUSION.

The general statistical table, appended hereto, gives the principal items of information, illustrating the progress of South Australia from its foundation. In glancing at this retrospect, one cannot fail to recognize the great success that has attended the enterprise of a handful of Englishmen, who, without adventitious aid, have, during a single generation, established a flourishing community, reproducing most of the social and material advantages of the Mother Country, and much of old world civilization, conducive to the happiness and prosperity of a people. Fifty thousand men, supporting thrice their number of women and children, occupy two hundred thousand square miles of pastoral country, and possess six millions of sheep; own six million acres of land, and grow twelve million bushels of wheat; conduct an external commerce of nine millions sterling, and raise one million of revenue. Such is the material result shown in the thirty-ninth year of the colonization of South Australia.

IGRA ON.	STAPLE PRODUCE EXPORTED.				SHIPPING, Inwards & Outwards.		RAIN-FALL.
l.	Total.	Breadstuffs.	Wool.	Minerals.	Number.	Tonnage.	
	£	£	£	£			Inches.
546	—	—	—	—	9	2,592	—
	—	—	—	—	—	—	—
477 42	5,040	—	770	—	—	—	—
,992 39	9,165	—	350	—	—	—	19·84
776 79	15,650	—	8,740	—	425	83,787	24·23
47	40,561	—	35,485	—	197	37,036	17·96
48	29,079	—	22,036	—	150	25,354	20·32
,213 58	66,160	—	45,568	127	104	15,533	17·19
,114 72	82,268	—	42,769	6,436	139	18,489	16·88
,336 59	131,800	—	72,235	19,020	225	26,558	18·83
,458 38	287,059	—	106,510	143,231	278	49,509	26·89
,645 48	275,115	—	56,130	174,017	301	62,641	27·61
,664 68	465,878	—	98,582	320,624	412	90,956	19·74
,166 53	373,842	—	108,539	219,775	549	155,920	25·44
,358 17	545,040	38,312	131,731	365,464	559	174,455	19·51
,464 87	540,962	73,359	148,036	310,916	538	155,002	30·63
,789 41	736,899	212,566	115,877	374,778	739	202,507	27·34
,128 14	731,595	257,144	236,020	176,744	869	260,917	27
,258 22	694,422	316,217	182,419	94,831	947	290,534	15·35
,211 15	686,953	236,400	283,479	155,557	711	225,923	23·15
,525 40	1,398,867	556,371	412,163	408,042	867	230,390	24·02
,138 72	1,744,184	755,840	504,520	458,839	970	282,368	21·16
,855 85	1,355,041	525,398	420,833	373,282	741	192,391	21·52
,869 76	1,502,165	554,265	484,977	411,018	792	216,128	14·85
,374 16	1,576,326	499,102	573,368	446,537	662	209,036	19·67
,127 11	1,838,639	712,789	623,007	452,172	788	199,331	25·19
,230 96	1,920,487	633,241	635,270	547,619	766	216,521	22·84
,234 17	2,095,356	747,116	715,935	542,393	886	255,493	22·92
,958 45	3,015,537	1,464,593	775,656	691,624	1,236	321,388	19·45
,169 46	2,754,657	1,228,480	821,482	620,112	1,220	357,290	14·75
,955 37	2,539,723	645,401	990,173	824,501	1,039	339,871	19·94
,651 22	2,776,095	1,037,085	919,532	753,413	1,136	343,819	19·35
,900 00	2,603,826	568,491	1,305,280	624,022	903	277,872	17·88
,807 35	2,722,438	890,343	1,008,696	627,152	1,112	333,507	13·85
,302 88	2,123,297	470,828	902,753	574,090	916	287,989	24·1
,532 97	3,289,861	1,253,429	1,170,885	648,509	1,238	373,624	23·5
,401 23	3,524,087	860,202	1,647,387	806,364	1,033	347,360	23·17
,548 59	4,285,191	1,711,746	1,617,588	770,590	1,531	515,640	21·6
,557 55	3,868,275	1,230,331	1,762,987	700,323	1,440	534,550	19·14
,593 51	4,442,100	1,680,996	1,833,519	762,386	1,634	611,381	31·45

☞ T 238,676,400 acres.

STATISTICAL VIEW SHOWING THE PROGRESS OF THE PROVINCE OF SOUTH AUSTRALIA SINCE ITS FOUNDATION.

STATISTICAL VIEW SHOWING THE PROGRESS OF THE PROVINCE OF SOUTH AUSTRALIA SINCE ITS FOUNDATION (continued).